POST BREXIT

Brexit Wounds

BOB BLIGHTY

IMPORTANT DISCLAIMER

The following is a work of satirical fiction, and not an actual description of true, real-life events. I mean, I'd have thought that was obvious, personally, but there you go.

All characters are completely fictional, apart from the ones who aren't. Even then, any living person referred to here hasn't done any of the things they do in this book. Or, not to my knowledge, at least.

It's made-up. It's not real. No need for outrage or death threats. It's just a bit of fun, OK?

Sheesh, you people.

Chapter 1

Rupert Sexton was a bastard. Always had been, always would be.

That was what he told himself during those long cold nights when he could hear the screams in the distance. That was what he reminded himself when he stumbled upon a gang of Bojos harassing some hapless victim, all giggling and guffawing beneath their masks and wigs.

And that was also how he justified it to himself when he turned and walked away.

He didn't care. He couldn't care. He was a bastard. Always had been. Always would be.

It had been a year since Britain left the EU. Around that, anyway. It was hard to know for sure, because once the TV and radio had shut off and the power had gone, keeping track of the date had begun to prove more difficult. Besides, knowing what day it was had quickly slipped way down most people's list of priorities.

Instead, that list had quickly gone back to basics. Food. Water. Shelter. Weapons. Those were the things you had to concern yourself with these days. Though, not necessarily in that order.

It was that first concern that Sexton was taking care of now. He stood knee-deep in the River Wey, the water burbling around him, moonlight playing across its ripples. Standing there, he could almost forget the remains of the burned-out KFC that lurked up the banking and across the road at his back, and the wider carnage of the world beyond.

The KFC had been an important stronghold in those early days, after the tunnel was closed and some legal bull-shit had prevented flights coming into the country. There were running battles to keep control of it for almost a full week after the UK crashed out of the EU. Same with the McDonald's a little further up the road. A lot of people had died in the fighting. Gammon-faced Brexiteers, mostly, who'd willfully ignored the advice to stockpile food and medical supplies, dismissing it all as 'Project Fear'.

"Fuck 'em," Sexton muttered, then he silently chastised himself as a fish that had been eyeing his improvised hook and line darted off through the murky water.

Three days after the Fast Food Wars had ended and the occupying armies had fully installed themselves, the food ran out at both premises. This prompted a resurgence in hostilities, in which both the KFC and McDonald's had been burned to the ground and several more Brexiteers had been killed.

Fuck 'em, said Sexton again, although only in his head, this time.

Of course, even with the fighting and the fires and the chaos, those early days now felt like halcyon times. The TV stations had gone out after a few days, but radio was still broadcasting, and much of the country still had power.

Back then, there was still a police force. Sure, there

wasn't a lot they could do to stem the rising tide of violence, but at least they still existed. The military, too, although those stationed abroad were unable to fly back in and could only watch from afar as the country tore itself apart.

They'd tried to drag Sexton himself out of retirement, but he'd made his feelings on that painfully clear to the armed 'recruitment officers' who'd come knocking, and packed them off again, relieved of their guns.

His house had been burned down shortly after. It could've been connected, but so many places were burning across the county it was most likely just a coincidence.

There was a movement in the water a few feet ahead of him. He saw himself reflected in the shimmering surface, and was a little taken aback once again by how the past year had aged him. He was barely over forty-five, but his greying hair and crows' feet suggested someone ten years older. The beard didn't help, but it had been a long, cold winter, and he'd been grateful for it at the time.

Sexton looked away from his reflection and focused on that flicker of movement. He held his breath, keeping the arm steady and his eyes on the prize.

The water was shallow here, but the darkness made it impossible to tell what the fish was. A Zander probably. They preferred these lower reaches of the river. Not a pike, he hoped. He still had the scar on his wrist from the last one.

Still, he'd take it.

He'd found the bait – a chunk of mouldy pork pie – in the wreckage of Aldi a couple of weeks ago. It was a small pie from a multipack that must've been kicked under one of the freezers during the initial wave of looting.

After scraping off the hairy blue clumps, he'd been hungry enough to try a nibble, but not so hungry that he didn't have the sense to quickly spit it out again. He'd seen people practically shitting themselves inside-out in recent months for eating similar floor-scrapings. But, by turning it into bait, that little pork pie had given him three meals so far, and hopefully now a fourth.

He felt the movement of the fish in the water.

Keep still. Don't tense. Not yet.

An engine roared somewhere in the distance. Across the river, up near the golf club, he thought. Not that it was an actual golf club these days, of course. It was a safe distance away, but the sound of an engine was such a rare one these days it almost shocked him enough to make his arm twitch.

Almost.

He remained motionless, only his eyes creeping down to follow the movement of the dull silver shape in the shallows.

Come on, you fishy bastard. Come on.

And then – yes! – a jiggle of the shoelace. The slightest tug as it jerked in his grip.

He thrust his other hand into the water, stealth no longer a concern. His fingers curved around the fish's underside and quickly gripped it before it could flap its way to freedom.

It broke the water with a look of utter indignation, its mouth gasping, its tail flicking like it could swim through air. Its back was silvery brown, mottled with dark spots. A trout! It was rare to find them at this end of the river, but Sexton wasn't about to complain. Guess it was just his lucky night.

"Evening, old boy."

Sexton froze. The voice had come from the river bank behind him. He'd been so fixated on the fish and trying so hard to not think about the engine sound that he hadn't been paying enough attention to what was happening behind him.

He could hear them now, quietly *umming* and *aahing* beneath their masks in that way they did. Four of them, at least. Probably more.

Stupid.

Stupid, stupid, stupid.

"What do you have there, my good chap?"

Sexton didn't turn. Not yet. He knew better than that.

"It's a fish. I caught it."

"Oh! Well, that's rather a spot of luck!"

The voice was muffled by the gasmask Sexton knew the owner would be wearing. He could picture the piggy eyes staring out through the circular lenses. God knew, he'd seen ones just like them often enough.

"Turn around, would you? There's a good chap."

Sexton turned, the water sloshing around his feet. The trout was still gasping but had stopped struggling. It, like Sexton himself, knew there was no point in resisting.

There were three of them standing in a line on the bank, a few feet apart, all dressed in variations on the theme of 'business suit' they'd cobbled together from Christ knew where. They all wore masks, most of them crudely fashioned from plastic or cloth.

The leader, of course, wore a full-face leather gasmask. They always did. Balanced on top of it was an unkempt wig of straw-like blonde hair – the trademark of a Bojo Squadron Leader. It was their equivalent of the Medal of Honour, and Sexton knew the guy would have had to have done some sick and depraved shit to earn those locks.

Four more, similarly dressed figures lurked behind the first three, a little farther up the bank and closer to the road. Sexton saw movement from the corner of his eye in the trees to his right, and heard the faint rustling of leaves in those to his left.

Surrounded. Nowhere to go, unless he tried swimming across the river. Even if he made it without being shot, what then? That was Grover territory, and those fuckers would stab him in the back before he'd managed to crawl his way out of the water.

He couldn't get past all the Bojos. Even if he could, their bikes would be propped up against the railings up there somewhere, ready to give chase.

"Be a good chap and say it, would you?" asked the leader. The way the moonlight played across his mask meant one side of his face was cast completely in shadow. An eye glared out through the lens on the other side, cold and cruel behind the glass.

Sexton sipped in a breath. The fish lay silent and still in his hands.

"She sells sea shells by the sea shore."

The Bojo leader tilted his head a fraction. The two beside him both leaned a little closer. The one on the left wore a knitted balaclava and sunglasses. The one on the right had cut eyeholes and a nose hole in the lid of an ice cream tub, then tied it on with string. He looked ridiculous, yet utterly sinister at the same time.

A year ago, these people would have been branded lunatics. Now, they were the law. Round these parts, at least.

"Again."

"She sells sea shells by the sea shore."

"And Pickled Peppers..."

"Peter Piper picked a peck of pickled peppers."

"And Sea Shells once more."

Sexton clenched his jaw, just for a moment.

"She sells sea shells by the sea shore."

The Bojo leader nodded, which made the wig slip forward on his head. He readjusted it. "Capital. Capital. Very good. Can't be too careful, can we, old boy? Don't know who might be doing the rounds."

He tapped the arm of the man in the ice-cream-lid mask and gestured to Sexton. "We shall, of course, be relieving you of the fish."

Sexton glanced down at the trout. An eye glared up at him. Accusing him. Taunting him.

He tore the paperclip hook from its mouth and handed the fish over without a word.

"And the line," said the Bojo boss.

Sexton hesitated then. It was only for a moment, but it was long enough that he heard the unsheathing of a long blade from the trees on his right.

He wound the shoelace into a loop, tucked the hook inside, then placed it in the outstretched hand of the plastic-masked Bojo. The eyes behind the mask held Sexton's gaze as the Bojo slipped the line into the breast pocket of his oversized suit jacket.

"Problem, old chap?" the man asked.

Sexton shook his head just once. "No," he said. "No problem."

"There's a good fellow," the Bojo said, before retreating up the banking to join the others.

The leader gave another nod, then readjusted his wig again. "Splendid. Splendid. Now that all that ghastly business is taken care of, we shall bid you a fond farewell. Thanks awfully for your co-operation, old boy. Best of British."

Sexton gave a nod. "Best of British."

The trees rustled on either side of Sexton as the lurking Bojos backed away. Those on the bank started to make their way back up toward the road, too, and the bikes that undoubtedly waited there for them. Sexton's racing heart rate slowed a little…

…then promptly picked up again when the Bojo in the balaclava whispered something to the leader, and they all stopped.

"I say, that's a very good point, old bean," the leader said. He turned to Sexton, and that eye peered out at him through the glass again. "He jolly well *is* out past curfew. That's rather rum luck for him, isn't it?"

The moonlight glinted on the lenses of the mask, turning them white. Behind the leader, the other Bojos produced knives and extending batons from the pockets of their suits. From the trees on Sexton's left, he heard the faint *click* of a gun safety catch being undone.

The Bojo boss's voice came as a sniggering guffaw. "Rather rum luck *indeed*."

Chapter 2

Sexton raised his hands, ignoring the weight of his own knife in his coat pocket. There were too many of them, too spaced out. Maybe if they didn't have the gun and he wasn't knee-deep in water and weeds...

But no. Even if he could fight back, even if he somehow won, what then? They'd find him eventually, then take their time killing him. Or worse, hand him over to the monsters in the NHS.

Better to take what was coming now, even if what was coming was a bullet through the skull and a watery final resting place. There were worse ways to go. Much worse.

And maybe it'd be for the best. What was left for him here? What was left for anyone? Pain. Fear. Hunger. Humiliation.

Oh sure, bananas could be bendy, and no-one was dictating the suction power of vacuum cleaners, but still. This was no life.

And yet…

"Please, don't," he heard himself say.

"Oh dear. You're not going to beg are you, old boy?

Strapping lad like you?" said the boss Bojo, his disappointment clear even through the mask. "Don't demean yourself. Where's your Blitz spirit? Where's your stiff upper lip? Take it like a man."

He nudged the Bojo in the balaclava, and indicated the Stanley knife the man clutched in one hand. "Bring me his eyes," said the leader. "Let the fish have the rest of him. Circle of life and whatnot."

Sexton brought his hands down, the weight in his pocket now too heavy to ignore. He heard the *bang* immediately and jolted, bracing himself for the pain.

But no. It wasn't a gunshot. The sound had come from up there on the street.

The Bojos turned as a Molotov cocktail exploded behind them, a spray of flame igniting the cheap Primark suit of the rearmost member of the group. He ran for the river, frantically slapping at himself as the fire licked up his front and melted the edges of his dented plastic mask.

A car engine roared. Tyres screeched. A woman cried out in a shriek of righteous fury.

"Fucking Tory scum!"

"Corbynites!" spat the lead Bojo, his plummy tones becoming much earthier. He shoved the Bojo in the ice-cream lid mask. "Well don't just fucking stand there, go get those neoliberal cunts!"

There was a clumsy scramble up the banking as the Bojos raced into action, Sexton all-but forgotten. He stood there, unmoving, as the Bojo who had been on fire heaved himself out of the Wey, adjusted his half-melted mask, then hurried after his companions, steam rising from the front of his ruined suit.

Sexton waited until they were all out of sight, listened to their angry shouts and the unmistakable *paff* off another

Molotov exploding on the ground, then quickly began to wade along the river, keeping close to the bank.

Another sound rang out. Definitely a gun this time, although more *boom* than *bang*, so most likely a shotgun. The tyres screeched again, most urgently than before. Shit, he didn't have long.

Pulling himself up onto the shore, Sexton ran along the riverside, forcing his way through the thin, spindly trees. There was no time to worry about being tracked. Besides, he didn't think they'd bother. If there were Corbynites in town then that would take priority over everything else, him included.

Still, best to get as far away from them as possible. Those bastards could be unpredictable, especially if their cages had been rattled.

He kept running until he passed under the road bridge that led across to the west side. The blockades were still in place – twisted tangles of scrap metal and barbed wire – so wherever the Corbynites had come from, they hadn't come this way.

Sexton waited under the bridge for a while, getting his breath back and listening for trouble. The car was still roaring through the streets, but farther away now and fading by the second. With any luck, the Bojos would be going after it.

But then again, luck had been in short supply lately.

He pressed on, cutting across the car park and through streets of boarded-up terraced houses, no doubt with families sleeping fitfully inside. He should head for home, he knew, try to get some shut-eye before the wake-up sirens. But he was still on edge, and he knew sleep was a long way off.

First, he had to calm down. And there was one thing he could always count on to do that.

———

SEXTON STOOD ON THE BEACH, listening to the whispering of the waves as they came creeping up the sand towards him. The wreckage of a fishing boat lay slouched on the sand behind him like the bones of some decaying dinosaur, blocking him from the sight of anyone who might come wandering along the Esplanade.

It was dark out there on the water, the moonlight barely skimming across its surface. He liked it at times like these. He could pretend that everything behind him didn't exist. He could imagine that he could see France in the distance, all vibrant and full of life. He'd spent a few weeks there with Alison, back before Brexit. Back before everything had gone to shit.

Back before she'd died in his arms.

He'd enjoyed it. France, that is, not the dying in his arms part. Paris had been so vivid and loud and... and *French*. They'd even done Disney, despite his protestations. He'd never got the chance to tell her that he'd secretly loved it.

He wondered what those across the water thought of them now. Did they know just how bad things had become? Were they laughing?

Not that he'd blame them. After all those months of negotiations that ultimately went nowhere, 'taking back control' had been the easy part. Maintaining it, however, had been something else, entirely.

No, he wouldn't blame them for laughing. The country was, after all, a fucking joke.

But this wasn't helping him calm down. He sat on the sand, closed his eyes, and let the sound of the waves wash over him. The wind coming in off the English Channel brought with it the last of the late-winter chill, and he zipped his jacket all the way up to his chin. It was a little small for him, but beggars couldn't be choosers. He'd worn it round the clock for most of the winter. He probably owed the thing his life.

The wind was warmer than it had been last week. Tomorrow, it'd be warmer still, teasing him with the hope of something better ahead. He knew better than to believe that, though. There was no happy future. No dream of some great tomorrow. There was just this. Always this. Day after day, week after week, year after year.

Post Brexit Britain.

"Should've let the fucking Bojos shoot me when I had the chance," he muttered.

A groan replied, and he clamped his mouth shut, cursing himself once again for speaking aloud. The sound had come from somewhere down the beach on his left, closer to the water.

He listened, praying it didn't come again.

But it did, just a moment later. Less a groan than a whimper, barely audible over the subtle swishing of the tide.

Fuck.

He shuffled quietly backwards until he was completely encased by the shadows of the wreck, his eyes fixed on the spot the sound had come from. It was probably an animal. That was it. A cat or dog whose luck had run out.

Or a bird, maybe. Yes. It'd be a bird. People were always trying to knock gulls out of the sky for food. One probably got clipped and then made its way back to the water before crash-landing here. A bird. Of course. That would be it.

And yet, now that his eyes were growing accustomed to that one particular spot, it was clear that the shape was bigger than a bird. Bigger than a cat, too.

A dog? Still a possibility.

Please, Sexon thought. *Let it be a dog.*

The sound came again – not a whimper this time, but a sob. Then a cough. Then the first few notes of what promised to be a good long cry.

Shit! Shit, shit, shit.

Sexton jumped up and stood, immobile, as his feet tried to run in opposite directions. He should get the fuck away, run up the beach, get onto the Esplanade then wind his way home through the back streets. That was what he should do.

No, that was what he was *going* to do. He was a bastard. Always had been, always would be.

But those sounds. That crying. It wasn't just a person lying out there. If it had been, it would've been easy. Sexton hated people, by and large, and he saw no reason to make an exception now.

But it wasn't just a person.

It was a child.

"Bollocks," Sexton spat, his left foot winning the battle and leading him in a crouched scamper down the beach in the direction of the cries. "Shh," he urged. "Shh, quiet."

He slid down into the sand beside the child. A head snapped around to him, eyes wide, mouth wider. It was a girl, eight or nine, maybe, long dark hair plastered to her face by water and wet sand. A three-inch gash ran across her hairline, blood oozing from it and painting her fore-head in a thin veneer of watery crimson.

She drew in a breath to scream again, but Sexton's hand clamped over her mouth, silencing her.

"Be *quiet*," he hissed, smothering her with his weight. "Someone will hear."

She stared at him over the top of his hand, eyes bulging, whole body shaking with cold and fear. He felt the warmth of her tears against his skin, but still he held on, pressing a finger to his own lips to signal that she shouldn't make a sound.

"OK?" he whispered. "Be *quiet*."

He gave it a moment to make sure she understood, then slowly withdrew his hand an inch or two, keeping it close in case he needed to clamp it over her face again. To his relief, she didn't scream. Just stared at him, silently sobbing as the blood trickled down over her face.

"Jesus Christ," Sexton muttered, settling back in the sand. "What are you doing out here? What happened? What's your name?"

The girl blinked several times.

"What's the matter, kid? You deaf? What's your name?"

"Gdzie ja jestem?" the girl whispered, and Sexton felt like the whole world suddenly gave way beneath him. He backed away, his arse carving a trench in the sand.

Oh no. Oh *shit*.

"J-Jestem martwy?" the girl said, the rising inflection in her voice indicating it was a question, the tears in her eyes suggesting it wasn't one she wanted to ask.

The accent was Eastern European. Polish, probably, although that was pretty much just a guess. Thick. Heavy. No disguising it.

She hissed and shrunk back against the sand when the beam of a torch hit her in the face, blinding her. Sexton spun up onto his knees. He caught a glimpse of several figures approaching from around the side of the boat wreck, but then the torch's beam was directed at his face, and his night vision was all-but obliterated.

"I say, chaps. Must be our lucky night."

Blinded or not, Sexton recognized the speaker. It was the Bojo Squadron Leader from earlier. He was out of breath, his voice fast and shaky through his gasmask. Sexton could practically hear the adrenaline coursing through it. That wasn't good.

The fact they'd found him was bad. The fact they'd found him here and now with this girl was infinitely worse.

"Good to see you again, old boy," the Bojo boss said. "And who's your little lady friend?"

"I don't know her," Sexton blurted. "I just… I heard crying. I came to check it out."

The Bojos stopped in a semi-circle around him. The one holding the torch directed it at his face, then the girl's, then back again, keeping him from seeing much. He could make out that the men all had their weapons drawn, though, and that was enough.

"Very public-spirited of you," the Bojo said. He applauded lightly and briefly, and with a definite undertone of sarcasm. "And they said the Big Society wouldn't work."

Folding his hands behind his back, the Bojo boss strolled around to the girl. He pulled the front of his trousers up an inch or two, revealing his blue socks, then crouched in the sand beside her. She shrank back at the sight of his mask, her tears coming faster than ever.

"What's your name, my dear?" the Bojo leader asked.

Sexton's heart crashed in his chest. He felt his throat go tight on the girl's behalf.

"Hmm?" the Bojo brushed the back of his hand across her sandy cheek, wiping a tear away. "What's your name?"

"Gdzie ja jestem?"

The Bojo boss's hand froze. A ripple of disgust went through the rest of the group, followed by some excited murmuring. Sexton closed his eyes.

No. God, no.

"I'm sorry, my dear? Would you mind awfully saying that again?"

The girl's eyes were like saucers now. The blood from her head wound meandered down her nose and dripped from the tip. It *paffed* gently into the sand. It should've been too quiet to hear, but it boomed like a thunderclap in the expectant hush.

"Gdzie ja jestem?" the girl whispered again, more slowly this time.

"Yes," said the Bojo. "Yes, that's what I thought you said."

She yelped in pain as he caught her by the hair and yanked her onto her feet. A *whoop* went up from the other Bojos. A few batons and machetes were *swished* excitedly.

"I say, chaps, it seems we have ourselves an interloping Johnny."

"Filthy foreign *muck*," spat the one in the balaclava.

"Bloody immigrants!" derided another.

"Hold up, hold up, not so fast, gentlemen," the leader said, chastising the others with a wag of his finger. "We shall do this properly, or not at all."

He turned his glassy gaze on the girl, still wriggling and squirming in his grip. "Would you be so kind as to say, 'She sells sea shells by the sea shore'? There's a good girl."

He chuckled, good-naturedly. "Rather appropriate, too, given where we are. Wouldn't you say?"

The girl looked up at him, eyes wide and imploring.

"SAY IT!" he roared, twisting his grip on her hair and forcing a sob from her lips.

She began to babble in Polish or Czech, or whatever the hell it was. The lead Bojo touched his mask where his ear would be and listened.

"You know, chaps, I think I detect something of an

accent there," he said, when her initial burst of babbling had faded. "All those in agreement?"

"Aye!" said the others in practiced unison.

"And those against?"

Silence.

Sexton rubbed both thumbs against the sides of his forefingers so hard the skin came off in greasy rolls.

A bastard. That's what he was. A bastard.

Always had been. Always would be.

"Motion carried. The Ayes have it," the Bojo boss said. "She's a Johnny, alright." His voice became a low, menacing whisper. "And we know what we do with Johnnies, don't we?"

The whooping went up again. The weapons swished. Sexton didn't meet the girl's eye. He couldn't.

Bastard.

Always had been.

"It's your lucky night, old boy," said the boss-man. "We've found ourselves some much better sport. Off you pop. But don't let us catch you out past curfew again, or you'll be in for a spanking."

He waved dismissively with his free arm. Sexton fixed his gaze on that hand and didn't look at the other one. Didn't study the way the fingers entwined through the girl's wet locks. Didn't dwell on the way the hand caressed the back of her skinny neck.

His feet wouldn't move. Not at first. With effort, though, he forced them to turn.

Bastard.

Always would be.

His legs felt heavy, but he heaved them up the beach, one step at a time.

The head Bojo's voice was an excited giggle behind him.

"Now then, young Johnny. Let's see what we'll make of you."

A knife blade flicked.

A child gasped.

A decision was made.

Sexton stopped.

Sexton turned.

The beam of the torch swung towards him. He caught the Bojo's wrist before the light could find him and twisted until something went *crack*. The Bojo ejected the beginnings of a scream, but a sharp jab to his throat trapped it in there somewhere, and he dropped to his knees, gasping and choking.

The torch landed in the sand beside him. Its beam flickered once, then went out.

"Give me the girl," Sexton said, his voice a growl in the darkness. "And everyone gets to live."

Chapter 3

They didn't give him the girl. Not that he'd been expecting them to, of course. Hoping, maybe, but it had definitely been a long-shot.

Two of the Bojos moved without any prompting from the boss. They were big lads, and moved with the sort of confidence that suggested they'd been in a scrap or two. They both had Union Flag dishcloths tied across the bottom half of their faces. They wore sunglasses, too.

Sunglasses.

In the middle of the night.

In the middle of a *fight*.

Silly bastards.

Sexton lunged with a kick that took out the first guy's knee. A right cross finished the job, spiralling the guy onto the sand.

Thrusting forward, Sexton drove the top of his head into second Bojo's nose. It hurt, but the sound of the bastard's nose crumpling and the choking sob that followed made any future lumps worthwhile.

"Don't just stand there, get the fucker!" snapped the boss-man.

The others sprang into life, but Sexton was already in full flow. He caught a knife that sliced towards him and wrenched it from the Bojo's grip. With a twist and a thrust, the blade found the underside of a plastic mask and a jaw. It tore easily through both, continued through the roof of the guy's mouth, and wedged somewhere in his nasal cavity.

Blood fountained from the wound when Sexton wrenched the knife free. He turned in time to deflect a baton and lunged forward with the knife, pressing both hands on the hilt as he shoved it through a blue tie and white shirt, burying it all the way up to the hilt.

The Bojo coughed and gasped behind his fabric mask. Sexton gave the blade a twist, then threw out a kick that doubled over another of the men who was rushing up behind him. It was the guy with the ice cream tub lid for a mask. Sexton caught the bottom of the lid and yanked it towards him. The Bojo screamed as the plastic cut through his nose, then stopped screaming when Sexton caught his head and twisted it much further than nature had ever intended.

There was no great style or extravagance to any of it. No flying kicks or spinning backhands. He moved with clinical, functional efficiency, taking each Bojo down as swiftly and brutally as possible, until only one was left standing.

"Move and I'll kill her!" the boss Bojo spat. He stood behind the girl, one hand still clutching her hair, the other pressing a knife blade to her throat. She stood rigid, her face frozen in a rictus of absolute terror.

Sexton knew exactly how she felt.

"Easy," he said, holding a hand up in a calming gesture.

"Don't facking 'easy' me, you prick!" the Bojo warned. The forced upper-class lilt was completely gone now, his accent switching to full-on *saarf London*. He gave the girl's head a jerk. "I'll do her, I facking swear!"

He shuffled around, keeping the girl in front of him, until his back was pointing up the beach. Sexton turned on the spot, keeping them both in sight.

The Bojo gave Sexton a quick up-and-down. "And you're dead, an' all," he spat, backing a few steps towards the Esplanade. "When I report this, when I tell the others what you've done, you're a facking dead man. You hear me? You're a facking dead—"

His heel found the body of one of his men, and panic flashed behind the lenses of his mask. The arm holding the knife came up as he tried to steady himself, stop himself falling.

Sexton struck. His knife broke one of the mask's round lenses, shattering the glass. He grabbed the girl and pulled her away, then grimaced as a flailing slash of the Bojo's blade caught him across the cheek.

And then the Squadron Leader crashed to the ground, twitching and convulsing, six inches of sharpened steel sticking out of his skull.

It was done.

It was over.

Well, almost.

Sexton placed a foot on the boss's neck and pulled the blade free with a *schlop*. Blood burbled up through the hole in the mask, then ran down into the lining of the wig that had landed on the sand beneath the masked head.

With knife in hand, Sexton approached one of the three men who were still breathing. He squatted beside him, then glanced back over his shoulder at the girl. "Turn around," he told her.

She stared back at him, not understanding. Or maybe she was going into shock.

Probably a little of both.

Straightening, he crossed to her and turned her by the shoulders until she faced the water. "These are bad men. *Bad men,*" he said, although he wasn't sure whose benefit that was for.

Once she was looking the other way, Sexton returned to the first of the injured men. He was on his back, blood oozing through his Union Flag tea towel from his shattered nose.

"P-please, don't," he gargled, dragging himself backwards through the sand on his elbow. "Please."

Sexton stood over him, the knife in his hand. "If it's any consolation," he said, dropping himself onto his haunches and adjusting his grip on the weapon. "I really am sorry."

And with that, he brought the blade down.

————

THIRTY SECONDS LATER, when the last of the Bojos was dead, Sexton placed the knife in a lifeless hand. It was unlikely the rest of the clan would buy that the guy had killed the rest of his squadron, then knifed himself through the heart, but it might confuse them for a while.

Of course, the tide would be coming in soon. If he was really lucky, it'd drag the bodies back out with it before anyone found them.

Yeah. Right.

Fishing in the pocket of the guy with the ice cream tub mask, he took back his fishing line. The fish itself was nowhere to be seen. Shame. That would've been a nice reward for…

For…

It was only then, standing in the circle of bodies, that the full enormity of what he had done hit him.

Not the killing part – Christ knew, he'd done enough of that to have made peace with it long ago – but *who* he'd killed. There would be reprisals. This would not go unpunished.

"Fuck," he spat, and the girl gave a little jump and a gasp of fright.

She still stood with her back to him, gaze pointed out in the direction she'd presumably come from. Sexton glanced past her into the darkness, but there were no lights out there beyond a faint orange haze near the horizon that he realised with a little jolt of shock must be France. He'd never noticed the light before, or the way it tinted the underside of the distant clouds.

Jesus. So close.

Sexton shook his head, dismissing the word 'swim' before it could fully take root. They'd all heard about the patrol boats out there, and how they shot swimmers on sight. No-one was able to agree on who the boats belonged to, but everyone was certain that they were there.

He would have dismissed it as scaremongering or propaganda had he not heard the far-off rattle of machine-gun fire on a few occasions, when the wind was low and the water still.

Sexton left while the girl's back was still turned, dabbing at the cut on his cheek as he padded up the beach. It wasn't long or deep, but it stung like a bastard. Probably the salt in the air.

He picked his way along the footprints the Bojos had left on the way down, covering his tracks as best he could.

The girl would be fine.

He stopped by the boat wreck and took a moment to check the coast was clear. If anyone had been watching from the Esplanade they'd have seen everything, but the front seemed deserted, most folks not daft enough to be wandering around past curfew.

She'd move. Eventually. It wasn't like she'd just stand there surrounded by bodies until someone found her.

He repeated his mantra, trying to convince himself of it.

Bastard. Always had been. Always would…

Ah, fuck.

Who was he trying to kid?

"Are you coming or—? *Jesus!*"

He jumped when he saw her standing just a pace or two behind him, wide eyes staring out from her curtain of wet hair. She didn't speak, just loomed there, tears streaming silently down her face, blood oozing from the cut on her forehead.

"Stay quiet. Stay close," he told her. He stole another glance up at the Esplanade, then sighed. "And for Christ's sake, do not say a *word*."

————

IT WAS ALWAYS a relief to get back to the house and find it still standing. There were far fewer fires these days – mostly because there wasn't as much to burn – but with no electricity and everyone relying on candles and camping stoves, they weren't exactly uncommon.

Sexton quickly undid the padlocks and pulled the wooden board aside, gesturing for the girl to go through. To her credit, and his relief, she'd stayed quiet the whole way back to the house, even when the Corbynites had come roaring past in their beat-up Ford Focus, screeching obscenities to the world in general.

She hesitated now, peering into the darkened gap between the wooden board and the doorframe, her feet shuffling anxiously in the overgrown grass. Fingers of light now crept across the sky, and the risk of them being spotted was growing by the second. He didn't have time for this.

"Go!" he barked, which only made her shuffle more nervously.

Grabbing her by the arm, he dragged her towards him. She shook her head, eyes widening again, mouth opening to scream.

"No, shh, it's OK," he said, immediately releasing his grip. He pointed into the opening. "Safe," he said. "Safe. Good." He tapped himself on the chest, then gestured to the building. "Home."

The girl's dancing became less agitated. Slowly, she extended a finger in the direction of the door. "Home?" she croaked.

"Yes! Yes, home!" Sexton said.

"Home?" she asked, still pointing.

"Yes! Yes. Jesus, what are you, E.T.?" he whispered. "Yes, home. Safe. Go."

He forced the gap open a little wider and beckoned for her to go through. Her eyes went from him to the narrow space, then back again. Finally, she ducked under his arm and scrambled through.

Sexton squeezed in after her, and she gasped as the board closed over and the darkness became absolute.

"Hold on, hold on," he told her, feeling for the box of matches he kept taped to the underside of the hall table.

After a moment of fumbling in the darkness, a match ignited, sending shadows scrambling across the graffiti-stained walls and over the yellowing ceiling. Sexton lit two candles with it, then shook it out and replaced the box.

That done, he closed the front door, fastened all three locks, and slid the chain across. Even if someone prised the plywood board off, it'd take them a while to get through the door. Long enough for him to do something about it, anyway.

It wasn't his house. Not in any legal sense, at least. But then, pretty much nobody lived in their own houses these days. Some banded together in little huddled communities, living six to a room because they felt that safety came in numbers.

The fires had reduced the overall amount of available housing stock, but once the purges had begun, all that changed. Anyone with a foreign-sounding name or, God forbid, a foreign accent had been dragged to the shore and forced to swim 'back home'.

Men. Women. Children. It didn't matter. If you weren't white English, you were rounded up and packed off. The lucky ones managed to take airbeds and armbands. The unlucky ones were chased into the surf, babies clutched to their chests, the mob howling and jeering at their backs.

A few Remainers tried to protest. A few who'd have once classed themselves as Leavers, too. But the mob mentality was running wild by then, and any resistance was swiftly and brutally stamped out.

After that, and with the ever-growing numbers of people choosing to huddle together, there had been plenty of houses to choose from. Sexton had settled on this one because its front door was tucked almost out of sight in the shadow of an old cherry blossom tree. Unless you were specifically looking for it, it was easy to miss. The back door and windows were weak-spots, but he'd barricaded them well, and anyone trying to break through had better be impervious to big fucking metal spikes on spring-loaded hinges.

Sexton picked up both candles and headed for the living room, gesturing with his head for the girl to follow. She hesitated at first, but as the pool of light ebbed away from her she hurried to keep up.

The living room was small but quite homely, provided you ignored the enormous 'FUCK EU, UK' that had been spray-painted onto one of the walls at some point before Sexton had moved in. Someone – possibly a different artist – had added twelve ejaculating cocks around the words in black Sharpie, mimicking the stars of the European Union's flag.

It was no Picasso, but Sexton had found himself coming to enjoy the installation all the same. The level of detail on the knobs alone was breath-taking. Veins. Pubes. Flying globs of spunk. Those dicks had it all.

And, like all great art, it posed questions. What was the intent of the slogan? Was it a straight 'fuck the EU' signed on behalf of the UK, or a more subtle, 'Fuck *you*, UK,' with the 'EU' part making the 'you' sound? Was it pro-Brexit, or anti? It was anyone's guess. He liked that. He also appreciated that they'd gone to the trouble of using a comma.

Other than the mural, and a layer of dust he'd never quite got around to cleaning, the room looked pretty much like any pre-Brexit living room had done. The curtains were drawn to hide the wooden board, and as long as you didn't pay attention to the half-dozen huge fucking spikes waiting to swing down and puncture the face of anyone stupid enough to jimmy open the window, it all appeared perfectly innocent.

Sexton indicated a cracked leather armchair. "Sit there," he said, placing one candle on the mantlepiece.

He didn't wait to see if she obeyed, and instead headed for the kitchen. He found the cleanest rag he could in the cupboard under the sink, dropped it into a bucket half-filled with gathered rain water, then rummaged in the drawers, searching for the box of sticking plasters he knew he'd seen there somewhere.

Aha!

Slipping the box of plasters into his pocket, he picked up the bucket, stepped over a collection of knives that stood blades-up in the middle of the floor, and then headed back through to the living room.

The girl stood on the same spot, shivering, water darkening the carpet around her feet.

"Why aren't you sitting?" Sexton asked, more harshly than he'd meant to. He set the candle on top of a pile of books beside the chair, then crouched and patted the seat. "Here. Sit."

After a moment, she sat. Sexton swirled the cloth around in the bucket a few times, wrung it out, then pressed it against the cut on her head. She flinched a little, but kept quiet, watching him silently with her wide brown eyes.

"Hold it," he instructed. When she didn't respond, he took her hand and replaced his own with it. "Keep the pressure on. Press. Press. OK?"

The girl said nothing.

"OK, then," Sexton sighed.

He stood up and moved to take the candle. The girl's eyes flashed with worry, so he took the one from the mantlepiece, instead. "Wait. I'll be back."

Leaving the room, he headed up the creaky staircase. It hadn't been creaky when he'd first moved in, but an afternoon with a claw hammer and a couple of screwdrivers had seen to that. Now every step squealed loudly in protest beneath his feet as he made his way to the upper landing.

There were three bedrooms. The one he slept in was down at the far end, the door closed. The door at this end stood invitingly ajar. There was a man-sized lump in the bed, made out of pillows. Inside the doorway was a large red rug that was just wide enough to cover a carefully cut hole positioned directly above the assortment of pointy things standing upright on the kitchen floor below.

Sexton stopped at the middle door. He'd only been in this room a couple of times since moving in, and wasn't relishing going in again.

He hesitated, one hand on the handle, dread tightening the tendons.

Needs must.

The door opened with a whisper as it brushed across the carpet. Perrie from *Little Mix*, winked suggestively at him as he entered. He only knew it was Perrie from *Little Mix* thanks to the text emblazoned across the bottom half of the poster.

Quite who the fuck *Little Mix* were, though, was anyone's guess.

The poster was above an unmade single bed, a deformed unicorn leaping clumsily across the crumpled duvet cover. There were a few teddies, but they sat neatly together on a chair in the corner, rather than tucked up in the bed. Remnants of a childhood on the brink of being left behind.

He had no idea what had happened to the girl who had been in this room. He wasn't sure he wanted to know, either.

There were clothes in the drawers and wardrobe. Probably all too big, but he bundled a selection over an arm, grabbed one of the cleaner towels from the bathroom, then headed downstairs.

The girl was still perched on the very front edge of the armchair, the cloth pressed against her forehead. It was as if she froze whenever he left the room. Just stopped existing whenever he wasn't around, then popped back when he returned, exactly as she'd left.

Sexton cleared some more books from the coffee table, used his sleeve to wipe away some of the dust, then set the clothes down. The girl's shivering was becoming violent now, her whole body trembling from top to toe.

"Here, let me see," he said, taking the cloth away and dabbing the edges of the cut. Cleaned up, it didn't look too bad. Smaller than it had first appeared. It was half an inch below the hairline, too, which meant he'd be able to get a plaster on it.

But first, she had to get out of those clothes.

Tossing the cloth into the bucket, Sexton indicated the bundle of dry garments on the table. "Get changed. Clothes. *Clothes*. Warm. Yes?" He sighed. "You don't understand a single word I'm saying."

He took a long-sleeved t-shirt from the top of the pile and held it out to her, waving it temptingly like a bullfighter's cape. "Clothes," he said again.

The girl blinked. "Clothes."

"Yes! Clothes! For you. Wear. Get dry. Get dressed. OK?"

He passed her the towel, then pointed to the kitchen. "I'll be through there. Shout me when you're ready and we'll get your head taped up."

The girl stared blankly at him, still shivering. He pointed to his forehead, before realising he was wasting his time.

"I'll be in the kitchen."

Once in the kitchen, Sexton leaned against the worktop and let himself sag, just for a moment. He'd had some shitty nights over the past year, but this one was shaping up to be up there with the worst of them.

Someone was going to find those Bojos, then someone would have to pay. He wasn't too worried about them pinning the killings on him, but they'd pin them on someone, and make everyone else watch as some 'good old-fashioned British justice' was meted out.

And then there was the girl. Fuck. What was he going to do there? He had no business bringing her back here. None. He saved her life. He'd done his part. He should've just left her.

Straightening, he arched his back and flexed his fingers, fighting back against the tension that had been building in his bones.

There was only one thing for it. Only one thing that could make this whole shitty mess better.

He popped the kettle on.

OK, technically it was a pot on a gas stove, but the principle was the same. He had a good stock of teabags left, but shared one between both mugs, dipping it into the first and swirling it around in the hot water for twenty seconds or so, before depositing the wet bag into his own mug and drowning it in water from the pot.

He tipped a couple of spoonfulls of sugar into the girl's cup. None in his own. There was no milk beyond the horrible powdered stuff, but he added a scoop of that to the sweetened mug, then took both mugs and hovered just inside the kitchen door.

"You ready?" he called through.

She didn't answer. He listened for the sound of movement, but heard none.

"Hey, kid. You ready?"

Nothing.

He risked a peek through into the living room. Both candles were still flickering, but there was no sign of the girl anywhere.

"What the hell?" Sexton muttered, stepping all the way into the room.

It was then that he saw her. She lay curled up on the floor, eyes bulging, hands pressed to her chest, breath coming in strained, shallow gulps. She'd made it into the t-shirt and a pair of jogging bottoms, both of which were so oversized they hung off her like robes. Her blue lips opened and closed fitfully, gasping and wheezing the way that fish had done earlier when it had been wrenched up out of the water.

"Aw," Sexton grimaced. "Shit."

Chapter 4

Sexton knew an asthma attack when he saw one, although this one looked worse than those he'd seen before.

After setting the mugs on the sideboard, he lifted the girl into the chair and propped her up against the back cushion.

"OK, calm. Calm," he said, soothingly. "I know, it's scary. But you can do this. You can breathe. In, out. You do it all the time, right?"

Her breathing was almost silent. He dimly remembered that this was bad. Better to be all rasping and wheezing than barely breathing at all. Her shivering had become a full-on shudder that wracked her skinny frame.

"An inhaler. Do you have an inhaler?" he asked. He mimed taking a puff from one, and thought she nodded, although the shaking made it difficult to tell. "You do? Where?"

He grabbed for the clothes she'd discarded on the floor and squeezed around the pockets. Empty.

"You don't have one. Did you lose it?" he asked, although she was clearly in no fit state to answer.

Shit. What else did he know about asthma attacks? Breathing into a paper bag? Or was that for panic?

He met the girl's wide, bulging eyes.

Yep, she was panicking, all right. Which was a damn shame, because he didn't have a paper bag.

What else?

"Trigger," Sexton said, the word appearing from the memory fog at the back of his mind.

He looked around them and winced a little at the layer of dust covering most of the surfaces. Motes swirled in the air from where he'd wiped the coffee table, dancing in the flickering candlelight.

He scooped her up in his arms, and she made no attempt to resist. She was lighter than she looked, and he barely noticed the weight as he carried her to the kitchen. He kept on top of the cleaning in there, and it was relatively dust-free.

Setting her down on the worktop, he motioned for her not to move.

"Wait."

He darted back to the living room, then returned a moment later with the cup of tea he'd made for her. "Here. Take this," he urged. "Drink. It'll help."

The girl's hands were trembling too much for her to hold the mug, so Sexton raised it to her lips. She managed a few sips, then a gulp, and while she wasn't instantly cured, her breathing at least became audible again.

Tea. Was there nothing it couldn't do?

"Good. That's it. You're doing great," he told her. "Just relax. Have some more tea."

By the time she'd finished the cup, her breathing was better. Not great, but better. Her shaking subsided, becoming just a low-level post-shock shiver of a type he'd seen a thousand times before.

"What's your name?" he asked her, once she seemed able to talk. Her eyes shimmered as she searched his face. "Your *name*?" he said, really sounding that second word out, much to his own annoyance. He'd always hated that 'Brits abroad' logic that if you just spoke slowly and loudly enough, non-English speakers would miraculously understand what you were trying to—?

"Marta," she said.

Jesus. It worked. It actually worked. Who knew?

"Marta. Hi." He tapped himself on the chest. "Rupert."

"Rupert."

"That's right. Rupert. You feeling OK?" He put his hand on his chest and mimed breathing. "OK?"

Marta nodded, although it was far from emphatic. "OK."

"OK. That's good. OK," Sexton said. He stepped back, giving her space. "What happened? Where did you come from? Was there… Were you on a boat?"

"Boat," the girl said. The way her face tightened and her eyes brimmed with tears gave Sexton an idea of the rest. "In water," she added.

"Oh. English. You speak English?"

Marta shook her head and held up a hand, finger and thumb placed close together to suggest a small amount.

"Do you know where you are?" Sexton asked her. He pointed to the ground at his feet. "You know where this is?"

Marta hesitated. "Francja?"

"You mean France? No," said Sexton. "England."

The look of horror on her face told him that yes, people in Europe did know what was going on here. Her already pale face turned ghostly-white. She shook her head and pressed herself against the wall behind her, her breathing becoming irregular and unsteady once more.

"It's OK. It's OK. You're safe," Sexton said.

A lie, yes, but a well-intentioned one.

"Home. Home. Please, home," the girl whimpered, her voice cracking. "Please."

"Look, calm down, OK? You need to breathe."

He watched her gasp and struggle, trying not to show his own rising levels of concern. The asthma was going to be a problem. Great. Like he didn't have enough already.

"You'll get home. I'll get you home."

Another lie. But what else could he say?

"But first, you need to rest. Sleep. Yes?" Sexton pressed his hands together and rested his head on them. "Sleep."

"Sleep?" said Marta, and Sexton wasn't sure if she didn't understand the word, or merely thought the very idea of being able to nod off right now was ludicrous.

She'd had a long night, though. They both had.

"There's a bed. Upstairs," he said, pointing up. Marta's eyes went to the ceiling, and quickly found the hole that had been cut there, directly above the upright blades.

"Don't worry. You won't be in that room," he told her. He lifted her down from the worktop and deposited her on the floor, slapping her bare feet on the lino.

"This way," he said, picking up the candle and beckoning for her to follow him. "And watch out for the knives. They're sharp."

———

AT THE TOP of the stairs, Sexton pulled the door to the first room closed. "Don't go in there, OK?" he said, scowling and waving his free hand in what he hoped was a suitably negative way. "No go in. Dangerous."

Marta nodded in what he hoped was understanding, and then shuffled after him into the next room. She glanced around at the soft toys and posters, then down at the unmade bed.

"You can sleep here tonight. Or today. Or… I don't know what time it is," Sexton told her. "We'll figure out what to do when you've had some rest."

Marta didn't move or give any indication that she'd even heard.

"Well, go on then," Sexton urged, jabbing a finger in the direction of the bed. "Get some sleep."

Marta shot him a worried look, then crept across to the bed. She slipped under the covers and pulled them all the way up to her chin, almost like a shield. She peered out at him from above it, concern drawing light creases on her face.

"Stay here, OK?" he told her. "Don't move. Unless someone comes in who isn't me. Then you run. Doesn't matter where to, just run."

Marta continued to stare. Sexton sighed. "You have no idea what I'm saying to you. Fine. Just stay. Sleep."

He set the candle on the dressing table and turned to leave, but the teddies on the chair caught his eye. He grabbed the closest one, gave it a quick brush down to remove some of the dust, and held it out to Marta.

She stared at it like it was some weird alien artefact, still cowering beneath the covers.

"You want it or not?" Sexton asked.

When she didn't reply, he started to withdraw the bear, but a hand came out from beneath the duvet and caught it by one dangling foot.

For a moment, they both held onto it, then Sexton nodded and released his grip. "There you go. OK. Get some rest. I have to go do something, but I'll be back soon."

He left the room and, with a final glance back at the girl, he quietly closed the door.

Right. So, that had been easy enough.

Now, for the hard part.

Chapter 5

"Well, well, well. If it ain't me old pal, Rupert the Bear."

Nigel's podgy, unshaven face cackled through the hole in the shutter, still amused by a joke he'd made dozens of times before.

"Bit early for you, ain't it? I ain't open."

Sexton adjusted a small rucksack he carried on his back and glanced in both directions along the street. The sun was still low but had started to filter through the clouds as it inched up the sky.

Another night survived.

"I need medicine," Sexton said.

"Why? You got crabs or something?" Nigel asked, snorting at his own comedy genius. "Got an itch in the old nether-nethers, have we?"

"I need…" Sexton leaned closer to the door and lowered his voice. He didn't think anyone was listening, but you couldn't be too careful. "I need an inhaler. You know, for asthma?"

Nigel scrutinized him through the gap in the corrugated iron shutter. "Asthma? What for? You ain't got asthma, has ya?"

Sexton nodded. "Since I was a kid. It doesn't flare up often."

"And what? It's flared up now, has it?" asked Nigel. His eyes narrowed, becoming two slits in a face like a slab of bacon products. "'Cos you look fine to me."

Sexton nodded. "It passed," he said. "But better safe than sorry."

"Just in case," said Nigel, nodding.

"Exactly."

"Right. Makes sense. 'Cept, you don't come hammering on my door before opening for a 'just in case' now, do ya?"

Sexton forced a smile through clenched teeth. "I guess I didn't realise the time," he said. "So, do you have one?"

"I got a lot of things."

Sexton waited until it became clear that Nigel was finished.

"Right. But do you have an inhaler?"

"Might do. But I ain't open. Come back after the alarm's gone and I'll see what I can—"

There was a sound, both terrifying and now utterly mundane. It rose like a chorus from the streets in all directions - the droning caterwaul of hand cranked air raid sirens.

"Jesus, they're sharp now, an' all," said Nigel, squinting out through the gap. "Wonder what's got them rattled?"

Sexton shrugged as nonchalantly as he could. An early alarm was never good.

"Don't know. Something in the air, maybe."

Nigel's eyes narrowed again. "Yeah. Maybe."

He sighed and muttered something as he stepped back

from the door and picked up the chains. "Fine. I suppose I'm open, then. Stand back."

Sexton retreated a couple of steps and waited for the shutter to finish rattling its way to the top of the door. There were windows on either side of the entrance, but they continued to enjoy the protection of their corrugated coverings.

"Well, fackin' come in, then," Nigel snapped, holding the door wide. "You're the one in the big rush."

Sexton stepped into the cluttered shop. He was immediately hit by a smell that he couldn't place, until he saw the Pot Noodle steaming on the counter, a fork sticking out through a gap at the edge of the foil lid.

"Bombay Bad Boy," said Nigel, clocking Sexton as he spotted it. "One of the few things the Pakis got right."

Sexton didn't know how to begin correcting that sentence, so he didn't even try.

"And no, before you ask, you can't fackin' have any!" Nigel cackled. He brought his fists up and mimed punching Sexton a few times, his red face reddening further with every laboured jab.

Sexton, for his part, didn't flinch.

The shop was one of only two left in town. Neither of them had any real theme beyond 'here's a lot of random shit that people need' but that was the only theme that really mattered in Post Brexit Britain, so they had both managed to thrive.

The place was an Aladdin's Cave of tinned foods, clothes, tools, books, and – most importantly – medicines. There was also a back store which Nigel referred to as 'Naughty Nigel's,' and where he kept a really quite breathtaking assortment of sex toys and porn.

Nigel himself was just under six feet tall – a little shorter than Sexton. He was heavier-set, though, and his easy regular access to food had added a layer of padding on top of his already bulky frame.

His head was shaved, but you didn't have to look too closely to see the male pattern baldness stubble that formed a horseshoe shape up top. He had that red-faced, slightly overcooked look that suggested either anger or alcohol issues.

There were tattoos on the backs of both his hands, both so badly faded by time and age that it was impossible to guess what they had once been, but it was a safe bet it hadn't been anything that might be considered complimentary to foreigners, women, or those of a homosexual persuasion.

Most of the wall space was taken up by shelving, but a spot had been reserved on the wall behind the counter for a large George Cross flag. It took pride of place, untouched by the clutter around it.

"What's going on?" asked a voice from through the back. A woman in her early thirties shuffled through, wearing a long shirt and a sleepy expression. Katie. Nigel's… what? Wife? Sister? Daughter? Sexton had never been able to figure it out.

Her hair was a silvery-blonde, cropped short enough to make her look either boyish or elf-like, depending on the angle.

"Oh. Sorry," she said, forcing her eyes open. "I didn't know anyone was—"

"Well they are," Nigel snapped. "So, go put some fackin' clothes on. The alarm's gone off."

Sexton doubted she need to be informed of this, since the alarm was still in the process of going off. The sirens continued their droning wail, determined that every poor bastard within earshot should be up and about.

"It's early today," Katie remarked.

Nigel caught Sexton's eye and sneered. "Hear that? Bright bitch, ain't she? Stephen Hawking eat yer fackin' heart out."

He turned on her, spitting the next few words out. "We know it's early. We ain't fackin' Irish. Now, go put some clothes on, you silly cow."

Katie opened her mouth to reply, then thought better of it. She briefly met Sexton's eye, then turned and vanished between the boxes of dildos and dog-eared back-issues of *Tits* and *Wank!* and *Big Busty Brits*.

"Silly cow," Nigel said again, though Sexton wasn't sure whose benefit it was for.

The wailing of the sirens faded into silence. Nigel rubbed his temples, mumbled a half-hearted, "Thank fack for that," then went behind the counter. He lifted the lid of the Pot Noodle, and inhaled the swirl of steam that rose from inside, savouring it as if it was the heady musk of the Lord God Himself.

"Christ, yes," he groaned, then he gave the contents a stir and folded the lid over again. He clapped his hands and rubbed them together. "Now then, Rupert the Bear," he said with a snigger. "What was it you wanted again?"

"An inhaler," Sexton said, which made Nigel draw in a sharp breath.

"Ooh. Yeah. Fack."

"You don't have one?" Sexton asked.

"Oh, no. I mean, yeah. I've got one. I've definitely got one," Nigel said. He placed his hands on the countertop and leaned forward a little. "But it ain't cheap. Who's it for?"

"I already told you. It's for me," Sexton said, but the way Nigel's eyes squinted and his nostrils flared said he smelled bullshit.

"You sure about that? It ain't for Tigger or Piglet?" He

properly cackled at that. Sexton frowned, not quite following at first. But then…

"That's Winnie the Pooh."

Nigel's brow furrowed. "You what?"

"That's not Rupert the Bear. It's Winnie the Pooh."

"No, it ain't. It's Rupert. With the red jumper."

"They've both got red jumpers," Sexton pointed out, then he changed the subject by swinging the bag off his shoulder and onto the counter top. Nigel's eyes flashed greedily. He licked his lips, salivating as much at the bag's potential haul as at the smell of his Bombay Bad Boy.

"Come on then. Whip it out for me, big lad," he said, snorting with barely contained laughter at his own comedy genius. "Let's see what you've brought yer old mate, Nige."

Sexton unzipped the rucksack and began offloading bashed tins of food onto the counter. Nigel's enthusiasm dulled as he watched the growing collection of cans. Corned beef. Spam. Rice pudding that was probably past its Best Before. Nothing startling.

"Is that it?" Nigel asked.

Sexton shook his head, then produced three books – two paperbacks and a hardback. Nigel prodded at them with affected disinterest. "Bit intellectual," he sniffed. "You ain't got that Fifty Shades tucked away in there, has ya? The birds are creaming themselves for it. Can't get enough of it, the dirty mares."

"No," said Sexton. He placed the bag on the floor beside him, making Nigel blink in surprise. "What? That's it?"

"What do you mean 'that's it'?" said Sexton. "That's a week's worth of food and a fortnight's worth of reading."

"But who the fack's going to read this?" asked Nigel, picking up one of the books. He held it at arm's length, like it might explode in his face, and cocked back his head to peer down his crooked nose at it. "*The Noise of Time*. I mean… what's that when it's at home?"

He dropped the book back onto the counter. "Nah. This ain't enough. Not nearly."

Sexton looked down at the stuff on the counter. "I can bring you more books."

"Fifty Shades?" asked Nigel, waggling his grey-flecked eyebrows suggestively. "Because if it's more of this high-brow bollocks, I ain't interested."

He gave a little gasp as a thought struck him. "Or, hold up. You don't have Tommy's book, do you? They're like fackin' gold dust."

Sexton picked up his bag. "Tommy who?"

"Robinson. Enemy of the State."

"Oh," said Sexton, adding '*that* nauseating cunt,' silently in his head. "No. Don't have it."

"Shame. Gold dust, they are. Fackin' gold dust."

Sexton loaded everything back into the bag, then looked down at himself. "What about the jacket? It's a good jacket."

Nigel sniffed, picked up his Pot Noodle, and gave it a stir. "Three months ago, maybe. The demand ain't the same now that we're headed into spring." He brought the fork to his mouth and noisily slurped up some of the soggy noodles, leaving a slick of sauce on his chin. His tongue came out, wriggling around like a fat purple slug as it licked the chin clean.

"Then what do you want?" Sexton asked.

Nigel shrugged and sneered at Sexton through the rising steam of his Bad Boy. "Surprise me."

A voice crackled from outside before Sexton could answer. It was amplified through a handheld loudspeaker and, Sexton guessed, muffled by a mask. Combined, these made it virtually unintelligible, but both men knew what it meant.

"Fack. What now?" Nigel wondered, setting down his Pot Noodle. "Katie!"

"I heard. Hang on," Katie called back.

"I'll fackin' 'hang on' you," Nigel barked. "Get a move on."

Sexton stepped out onto the street, swinging the bag up onto his back. Four Bojos stood in the middle of the road, well spread out, two facing one side, two facing the other. Their suits and masks were higher quality than the ones he'd crossed paths with in the night, although none of them wore the tell-tale wig of a leader. One of the men facing Sexton's side of the street held the loudspeaker up near his head, his finger on the trigger. His head was encased by a black leather mask with a zip for the mouth, which he'd pulled open.

A few other people came crawling out from gaps in boarded-up doorways. Some filed out from the side-alleys, silent and sheepish, eyes flitting anxiously from mask to mask. The mangled sounds of other amplified announcements came from all directions. This was a full-town wake-up, and that could only mean one thing.

The Bojo with the loudhailer raised it to the lips of his smooth plastic mask. "Thank you for your prompt responses," he said. Or something resembling those words, at least.

He paused, as if waiting for a response, but well aware he wasn't going to get one. "Doubtless, you are all wondering just what all the fuss is about," the Bojo continued. "I'm afraid I have some rather bad news."

Nigel and Katie stepped out of the shop and fell into line beside Sexton. He glanced at Katie, just briefly, then turned his attention back to the main event.

"It seems a squadron of Bojos – ruddy fine chaps, too – was murdered last night. Rather brutally, too."

There were forty or more people gathered along both sides of the street now. None of them uttered a sound, but the worry was write large on their faces for all to see.

"And, of course," crackled the Bojo. "We simply cannot be having that. Can we?"

He waited for a reaction. "*Can we?*"

A murmur went around the audience that seemed to agree that no, they couldn't be having that.

"No. We can't. That's why the Man Himself is being informed," the Bojo continued. He paused again, letting that sink in. In the lull, Sexton could hear several similar announcements taking place in the adjoining streets.

"What, *the* Man Himself?" said Nigel.

"Indeed, old boy," said the Bojo. "The original and best. We shall await his proclamation with baited breath. But before then, of course…" He glanced along the row of onlookers before him. "…there will be a reprisal."

Sexton heard someone sob. He didn't turn to look.

"Several reprisals, actually," the Bojo continued. He sighed. "It's a ghastly business but, alas, a necessary one, as I'm sure you will all understand. Can't have anarchy now, can we? Where would we be? In a right ruddy mess, that's where.

"Of course, the number and severity of these reprisals can be mitigated somewhat if the brute responsible owns up," said the Bojo, peering out through the eyeholes of his gimp mask. "From what we can tell, he's a big chap. Had a little kiddie with him. They walked up the beach together, headed this way. We have footprints and a witness statement to corroborate that."

A witness statement? Shit. Oh, *shit*.

But, no. There had been no-one around. He was sure of it. They were bluffing.

From the corner of his eye, Sexton saw Nigel turn his head, scrutinizing him. He kept his own gaze straight ahead on the Bojo, trying to appear exactly as worried as everyone else on the street. No more, no less.

"Ringing any bells?" asked the Bojo. He paused a moment, leaving a space for anyone who felt particularly suicidal to step in. No-one moved or said a word.

"Well, we'll just have to do it the hard way, won't we?" the Bojo said, not bothering with the loudhailer this time. "Looks like we're having a Day of Reckoning."

He gave that a few seconds to sink in, too, then placed the megaphone to his mouth and pressed the trigger. "Dismissed. But don't try to go anywhere. Cordons are in place. The Reckoning will begin in a few hours. Attendance, as ever, is mandatory. There's good chaps."

The Bojo lowered the loudhailer, and all four of them motioned for the crowds to disperse. Sexton could still feel Nigel's gaze on him but did his best to pretend that he didn't. Turning, he walked off along the pavement, pulling his bag higher up onto his shoulder and lowering his head against the early-morning drizzle as it started to fall.

Chapter 6

Marta was asleep when Sexton returned to the house, having apparently slept through the air-raid siren wake-up call, and the screeching of every step as Sexton had made his way up the stairs to check on her. Poor kid must be exhausted. No wonder.

There was a faint whistle to her breathing from deep within her chest. It sent Sexton looking through the house for items of value that Nigel might take in exchange for the inhaler.

The problem was, Sexton lived a pretty Spartan life-style, with little in the way of luxuries beyond books. The house had been pretty much stripped of anything valuable before he'd moved in, and he'd already traded most of what was left over for toothpaste and soap. If Nigel wasn't willing to accept food or books, there wasn't a lot else Sexton could offer.

He found his untouched mug of tea while searching the living room for anything trade-worthy, then tipped it down the kitchen sink and made himself another.

Returning to the living room, he sat on the armchair to

drink it. Although it was light outside, the boards on the windows kept the place dark. Sexton sipped his tea and watched the flickering candlelight shadows dance up and down the walls.

A mote of dust drifted in front of him. His eyes followed it as he slurped from his mug, watching as it floated lazily through the pool of light, then vanished into the darkness beyond the candle's reach.

Looking down, he gave the arm of the chair a pat, and watched as the air around it became alive with dust.

"Bollocks," he muttered, then he downed the rest of his tea in one.

———

AN HOUR LATER, Sexton dropped the cloth into the bucket of grimy water and admired his handiwork. The coffee table, sideboard, and all solid surfaces were now dust-free. The armchair, being leather, had been easy enough, but the couch – a slouching green fabric monstrosity made almost entirely of cushions – had been more of a challenge. He'd just have to make sure the girl didn't sit on that.

Which meant giving up his armchair.

Great. Like she hadn't messed his life up enough.

Sexton was about to reward all his hard work with a nice cup of tea when someone knocked at the door. He ducked, instinctively, and spun in the direction of the sound.

What the hell was this? No-one ever came knocking. Why would they be starting now?

Shit.

He waited, hoping it was a one-off. An anomaly. A glitch in the fucking Matrix.

But, no.

It wasn't loud, particularly, but it was insistent – an urgent *ratatatat* on the board that barricaded the back door. He'd seen the Bojos knocking on doors before, and it didn't sound anything like that.

Still, better safe than sorry.

He fetched his knife from inside his jacket, held it low and ready, then approached the door. The locks and chain were back in place, securing it from the inside.

Sexton listened for a moment, staring at the peeling gloss paint on the door as if he could somehow see right through it.

The knocking came again. Low. Urgent.

Ratatatatat.

"Who is it?" he asked.

The knocking stopped. "It's, uh, it's Katie," came the reply. "From… from the shop."

Sexton's grip tightened on the knife. "How did you find me?"

"Nigel had me follow you. Before, I mean. Not today. He doesn't know I'm here."

"He had you follow me?" Sexton snapped, worry twisting his guts. "Why?"

"He has me follow most of his customers," Katie replied. "He says it's in case anyone tries to screw him over."

Sexton looked to the ceiling, recalling the way Nigel had watched him outside the shop earlier. He glanced up the staircase behind him.

Fuck. This could be a problem.

"What do you want?" Sexton demanded.

"Can I come in?" Katie asked.

"No. What do you want?"

"It's… I brought you the inhaler."

Sexton frowned, caught off guard. "Why?"

"Well, because you said you needed it," Katie replied. "Look, I don't really want anyone to see me out here. Can you open the door?"

"Leave it on the step," Sexton said.

Even through the barricade, he heard Katie sigh. "Seriously? You know what I'm risking bringing you this fucking thing?"

Her voice changed, coming from lower down the door. "Fine. It's on the step. Enjoy."

Sexton pressed his ear to the wood and listened to her walking away.

A moment later, she returned.

"Oh, and you're fucking welcome, by the way."

He heard her make to leave again.

"Wait," he told her. "Hold on."

He unfastened the locks and unhooked the chain, but kept the knife ready as he opened the door. A thin, watery sunlight seeped in through the gap beneath the board. He pushed it outward at the bottom corner with his foot.

"You'll have to crawl in," he instructed.

Her own feet appeared first, then she squatted and craned her neck to see in. She wore a thin jacket, the kind summer campers packed rolled-up in rucksacks, just in case. The drizzle had slicked her fringe to her forehead, and she blew a drip off the end of her nose before smiling up at him.

"Hi. Thanks."

"Hurry up," Sexton urged, standing aside so she could crawl through.

"Right, yeah. Hang on."

She clambered awkwardly through on her hands and knees. Sexton was hit by a shake of water spray as she stood up and pushed back her hood. Her face was red, like she'd been running.

"Did anyone see you?" Sexton asked, closing the door at her back.

"I fucking hope not, or I'm deep in the shit."

She held out a blue plastic inhaler. "Here. Hope this is the right one, because it's the only one I could find."

Sexton took it from her, turned it over in his hands a couple of times, then nodded. "Thanks. Won't he notice it's missing?"

"Not if you don't come asking for it again," Katie said. "So, you know, don't do that."

"Right. No. I won't." He put the inhaler in his pocket. "Thanks again."

"No problem," said Katie. "Also, please don't stab me. That would be unpleasant."

Sexton looked down, remembering the knife in his hand. "Right. Sorry." He slid the blade between his belt and the top of his trousers, so it ran down the side of his hip.

"Can't be too careful," Katie said. She opened her jacket to reveal a knife of her own. It was sewn into the inner lining so only the handle and the top half-inch of a sheath protruded.

"Right," Sexton agreed. "Can't be too careful."

He placed a hand on the door handle. "So, thanks again for the inhaler. It's really kind of—"

Sexton stopped when he saw the girl at the top of the stairs. Or, more specifically, when he saw Katie seeing the girl at the top of the stairs.

Katie stared up at Marta, her mouth creaking open as if in slow motion.

"She's my daughter," Sexton blurted.

Katie side-eyed him. "You have a daughter?"

"Yes. Evidently. Haha. So… Yeah. That's it. She's my daughter."

"Jestem spragniona."

Katie gasped.

Sexton sighed.

There was a *clunk* as he turned the lock on the door.

"Shit. No!" said Katie. "What? I mean… *What?* She's not…? No! She can't be… *No!* Can she?"

The pieces suddenly clicked into place and she gasped again, louder this time. "The Bojos! That wasn't…? Was that…?" She looked Sexton up and down, then squinted up the stairs at the girl again. "No! She couldn't have…"

A third gasp, the loudest of all. Katie spun to face Sexton. "You! Did you…? You know. The Bojos? *Did* you? Shit. Ooh, shit."

"No. I don't know what you're talking about," Sexton insisted. "Whatever you're thinking – whatever you're trying unsuccessfully to say – stop. Just stop."

He forced a smile and glared meaningfully at Marta, still trying to salvage this. "Uh, honey? You go back to bed, OK? Be a good girl for daddy."

Marta blinked, confused. "Nie rozumiem."

Sexton attempted a laugh. "Ahaha. Good one, honey. But remember what I told you about pretending to speak that weird foreign crap? Some people won't find it as funny as—"

"I'm not buying it," said Katie.

Sexton's smile fell off. "No. No, I didn't think you were," he conceded.

"Admirable attempt, though," Katie told him. "Seriously, good try."

She clicked her fingers a few times, danced on the spot, then sat on one of the lower stairs. It squealed in protest.

"So," she said. "What now?"

"I don't know," Sexton replied.

"You're wondering if you can let me leave. You're probably worried I'll grass you up," Katie said.

"That had crossed my mind."

"Well, I won't. I promise."

Sexton shrugged. "Sorry, but that's not exactly worth much these days."

"It's the only thing worth anything," Katie corrected. "Look. The only way I could know about her is if I came here. Right? And if Nigel finds out I came here then… Well, let's just say I don't want that."

"Who is he?" Sexton asked, intrigue getting the better of him. "To you, I mean?"

Katie shrugged. "No-one, really. A friend of the family back from before." She shifted on the step, eliciting a chorus of creaks. "My parents were in Wales when the old nuclear plant went up. Trawsfy… Whatever."

Sexton gave a nod. "Sorry."

"It is what it is," said Katie, clearly having made her peace with it. "I had nowhere to go, he had food and seemed to be OK, so… Yeah. I've been there since. He wasn't always like he is now."

She shrugged. "Or, you know, maybe he was, but just hid it better. No-one bothers to hide it these days."

The stairs creaked as Marta padded down the top few. Katie turned and knelt on the step she'd been sitting on. She smiled at the girl and gave a little wave. It took Marta a moment, but she eventually waved back.

"Hi there! I'm Katie. What's your name, sweetheart?"

"It's Marta," said Sexton.

"Check it out. You can throw your voice and sound like a man," Katie said. She pulled a face, which made a smile tug at one corner of Marta's mouth, then held her hand out. "Well, it's very nice to meet you, Marta. We don't get to see many new faces around here."

Marta hesitantly took the offered hand and shook it. Katie beamed, looking genuinely delighted that the girl had accepted the gesture.

"Has she eaten?" Katie asked, looking back over her shoulder.

"Yes. Wait. No," said Sexton. "She had tea."

"Just tea? That's it?"

"She's been sleeping," said Sexton, suffering a sudden pang of guilt. "She was tired."

Katie stood and unzipped her jacket all the way. "Right. Where's the kitchen?"

Sexton frowned. "What? No, I can…"

"I've got half an hour until Nigel starts wondering where I am," she said, holding up a hand to silence him. She removed her jacket and hung it on the hook by the door, then looked around the hallway and jabbed a thumb in the direction of the single interior door. "So, kitchen? I'm guessing it's this way?"

———

SEXTON LEANED against the kitchen worktop, wondering what the hell to do. Katie was sitting on one of the four rickety kitchen chairs, watching Marta slurp Super Noodles from a chipped bowl. She hoovered them up, more inhaling the food than actually eating it.

"See?" grinned Katie, looking back at him over her shoulder. "Told you she was hungry."

Marta's eyes raised and looked at them both for a moment, then turned their attention back to the matter at hand.

"It's very noodle-based, isn't it?" Katie said.

Sexton frowned. "What? The noodles?"

"No, I mean food in general. Nowadays. There's a lot of noodles involved. Pot Noodle. Super Noodles. Those little fake Super Noodles. Pretty ironic."

"Why is it ironic?" asked Sexton, not following.

"Well, I mean, they're not exactly British, are they?" said Katie, turning so she was sitting side-on on the chair. "They're Chinese. It's just surprising, the way everyone talks about foreign stuff these days. It's just surprising that they're still around."

Sexton shrugged. He'd never really given it any consideration. "Half of them believe we invented curry. I wouldn't overthink it."

Katie's eyes fell on the assortment of knives on the floor, then crept up to the hole in the ceiling. She snorted out a little laugh, as she understood the significance of both elements.

"So, what's your plan?" she asked.

"What do you mean?"

"Well, you can't stay around here, can you? What if they find her?"

Sexton crossed his arms. "And where am I supposed to go, exactly?"

"Well, not here! The Bojos are looking for her. For both of you. You can't stick around here, or they'll find you."

"What am I supposed to do?" asked Sexton. "It's not like I can just take her back. Even if I had a boat – which I don't – we wouldn't get past the gunships."

Katie rolled her eyes. "Well, *obviously* you don't go across the Channel."

"Obviously."

"You go north."

The furrows on Sexton's brow deepened. "London?"

"No, *north* north. Scotland."

"Scotland?"

"You know, the country? Kilts. Haggis. Social justice and fairness for all. That stuff," Katie said. "I bet they'd take her."

Sexton uncrossed his arms, crossed them again, then shook his head. "No. That's… It's too far. We wouldn't make it."

"We would if we were careful," Katie said.

"No, it's…" Sexton blinked. "What do you mean, 'we'?"

"I thought I'd come with you," Katie said.

"Well, you thought wrong. Anyway, we're not going, so—"

THUD-THUD-THUD.

Sexton straightened sharply, the blood draining from his face, fear and anger and everything in between twisting his gut.

Now *that* – that was a Bojo knock.

Chapter 7

"You fucking liar," Sexton spat, grabbing for the knife in his belt. "You set us up."

Katie jumped up, shaking her head. "No. It's not me. It wasn't me. I swear!"

THUMP-THUMP-THUMP.

"Open up, old boy!" crackled a voice from outside. "We'd like a quick word."

"I don't believe you," Sexton snarled. "This was you."

"No. It wasn't," Katie insisted. "But they're going to come in."

She spun and grabbed for Marta, who had raised her head from the bowl and paused, fork halfway to her mouth. The fork clattered onto the table as Katie dragged her to her feet, pressing a finger to her lips, urging her to keep quiet.

Turning, Katie saw Sexton take a second knife from a drawer. "What are you doing? You can't just kill them all!"

BOOM-BOOM-BOOM.

"Come out, come out, wherever you are!"

"Want a bet?" Sexton said.

"That's insane. I have an idea. Do you trust me?"

Sexton shook his head. "No."

"Well, tough shit. Come on."

She hurried through into the living room, pulling Marta behind her. Marta didn't struggle, and didn't make a sound as they crept through into the hall. Katie was about to step onto the staircase, but Sexton caught her arm and signalled for her to wait.

They stood there, all three of them holding their breath.

BANG.

The wooden board rattled against the door as something hard and heavy battered against it. Sexton urged Katie up the stairs. They raced to the top, the banging on the barricade disguising the creaks and squeals.

"Where's your bedroom?" Katie asked. She pointed to the first door. "This one?"

"No! Down there, but there's no way out. We won't get the window open in time," Sexton said.

"We don't need to."

They hurried across the landing, before Katie skidded to a stop. "Wait. Where did Marta sleep?"

"In there," said Sexton, nodding to the middle door. "Why?"

"Shit. OK. In here, then." Katie dragged Marta into the room and immediately dropped to the floor next to the bed. "Fuck. It's going to be tight."

Downstairs, wood splintered. Katie caught Marta by the arms. "Marta, honey. You need to hide, OK? Under the bed."

She pulled the girl down to floor level. Marta's eyes were wide and staring.

"She doesn't understand," Sexton began, but then

Katie lifted the single bed a few inches and Marta squeezed underneath.

"Yes, she does." Katie leaned down and pressed her hands tight over her ears. "Don't listen, OK?" She screwed her eyes shut and pressed harder, then shot Marta an imploring look. "Got it?"

"Bad men, Marta," Sexton added. "Bad men."

Marta brought up her hands and placed them over her ears, then closed her eyes. "Good girl."

"Great. Now what? That's your plan? Hide her under the bed? That's it?" Sexton hissed, his voice almost drowned out by the hammering of a battering ram, and the *crack* of breaking wood.

"No, that's not it. Take your clothes off," Katie urged, undoing her belt buckle and kicking off her trainers.

Sexton blinked. "What?"

Katie stomped out of her jeans and pulled her shirt up over her head, revealing a mismatched set of underwear. Sexton watched on, dumbstruck, as she quickly pulled those off, too. Naked, she jumped into bed.

"Clothes. Hurry the fuck up!"

Sexton glanced at the gap below the bed, then undid his belt and hurriedly stripped down to his boxers.

"Pants, too!" Katie hissed, just as a thunderous *ker-ack* from downstairs signalled the door giving way.

Sexton dropped his kecks and jumped into bed, just as Katie let out a high-pitched squeal of excitement. She pushed him onto his back and straddled him, back arching, hands on his chest.

"Yes! Fuck!" she yelped, then she glared down at him and placed his hands on her hips. "Well don't just lie there like a sack of potatoes," she whispered, before resuming her orgasmic writhing and groaning.

It took a lot to surprise Rupert Sexton. He'd made a

career out of dealing with the unexpected, then survived the last year by being ready for anything.

This, though. This now? This he hadn't seen coming.

From out on the staircase came the thudding and squeaking of footsteps.

"Yes! Yes, baby! Yes!" Katie gasped. She shot Sexton a glare and he finally joined in with the act, grunting and thrusting, trying very hard not to think about the girl hiding just a foot below them.

Jesus, he hoped she still had her hands over her ears.

The door flew open, revealing three Bojos, each holding machetes. Katie screamed, slid off Sexton and scrabbled to hide her nakedness beneath the covers. It was a single bed, so most of her was still pressed against most of Sexton. Her warmth and the softness of her skin briefly rendered him mute.

"What the *fuck*?" she yelped. "What's going on?"

"Uh, yeah. What is this?" Sexton added, finally finding his voice. "What's all this about?"

The Bojo in front regarded them through the lenses of his gasmask. He wore the blonde wig of authority, and – if Sexton didn't know better – could easily have been the squadron leader from the night before.

With a nudge, the Bojo boss sent his two accomplices away. "Go and look."

They nodded and retreated out onto the landing.

"Wait!" Sexton said.

The Bojos stopped.

"The, uh, the room on that side is booby-trapped. You know, in case of looters? Don't stand on the rug or you'll fall through."

The head Bojo glowered at him for a moment, then nodded. "You heard him. Avoid the rug. But check it."

"You can't just come barging in here," Katie said.

"We can, my dear," said the Bojo in those forced plummy tones. "By orders of the Man Himself. At officially-recognised times of great crisis, we have the power to go anywhere we please."

"And who gets to officially recognise it?" Katie asked.

"Ha. Who, indeed?" the Bojo replied. He looked around the room, then used the tip of his machete to pick up Katie's discarded bra.

For a moment, he regarded it in silence, then he flicked it at her. It landed on the unicorn bedcover. "Get dressed. Both of you," the Bojo ordered. He backed into the hall. From downstairs, there came the crash of furniture being turned over.

The Bojo boss caught the door handle, looked briefly around the compact room again, then started to close the door. "And don't keep me waiting. There's good chaps."

———

SEXTON AND KATIE sat on the couch, listening to the thumping and thudding from the other rooms of the house. The coffee table had been broken. The sideboard upended. Sexton hadn't been allowed to look in the kitchen yet, but he assumed it would be much the same.

The Bojo boss sat in the armchair, one leg crossed over the other, the blade of his machete resting on his knee. The lenses of his gasmask were tinted, making it impossible to see his eyes. He remained almost perfectly still, the *click* of his breathing through the filter the only indication that he was still alive.

Two others stood on either side of the armchair, their own weapons lowered, but held in a way designed to make it clear that it would be no problem to raise them again.

"Maybe if you tell us what you're looking for," said Sexton. "We could help."

"That won't be necessary," the Bojo boss said. At least, the voice came from his direction, but his lack of movement seemed to disconnect it from him. "We know what we're doing. Thanks awfully for the offer, though."

Sexton leaned back in the chair, heard another crash from upstairs, and leaned forward again. He rested his elbows on his thighs, forcing his legs to stop bouncing.

Katie sat beside him, just a few inches gap between them. She'd made him look away while she'd got dressed, which felt little like shutting the stable door after the horse had already bolted, but he'd been quick to oblige.

"Was it Nigel? Did he send you?" Katie asked.

The Bojo remained motionless and impassive behind his mask.

"Because if it was him, you should know that he's jealous. He's got this idea that we – that me and him… And, you know, just – ew. Fuck. No. I've told him it isn't happening, but he just can't let it go. When he heard about me and Rupert, I just knew he would—"

"Do shut up," the boss-man said. A tension hung like an aura around him for a few seconds, then he tapped his knee with the flat of the machete blade, breaking the spell. "There's a good girl."

They sat, not speaking, as the thumping continued upstairs. There was a loud *crash* from directly above them. Sexton's own bedroom. Probably the wardrobe coming down. He *cricked* his neck a little but didn't voice any objections.

The floorboards on the landing squeaked as someone moved across the landing. Sexton chewed his bottom lip, breathing through his nose, the three Bojos watching him in silence.

And then footsteps were moving down the stairs, and two other Bojos entered the room. They were empty handed, other than their long, curved knives. Sexton tried not to show his relief.

He and Katie both watched on as one of the Bojos crossed to the boss, bent down, and whispered softly in his ear. The whispers echoed weirdly behind the rigid plastic mask he wore. It was one of those masks you could pick up from craft shops to decorate yourself, only this guy hadn't bothered to get creative with it.

Sexton felt Katie's hand slip into his as the whispering continued. He wasn't sure if it was part of the act or not.

"I see," said the boss Bojo, once the other man straightened.

He said nothing more for a while, and just tapped the flat of the machete blade on his knee.

Five of them. All similarly armed. Four close together, one over by the door. The couch was low, the cushions soft. Four of the men were already standing.

It wouldn't be easy. Doable, though.

"Where is the child?" the boss-man asked.

"Wait. You have a kid?" Katie gasped, pulling her hand away from Sexton's. "Since when did you have a kid?"

"Huh?"

"I thought you said that bedroom was from the people before?" said Katie, looking utterly indignant.

"It was. It is. It… No. I don't have a kid." Sexton turned to the Bojo. "I don't have a kid. What kid?"

"We were informed that you had *acquired* one, dear boy." The leader leaned forward in the chair, the leather groaning beneath him. "Have you?"

Sexton shook his head. "No. I mean, how do you acquire a child?"

"Where were you last night, Mr. Sexton?"

Katie slipped her arm through Sexton's. "He was with me. We were together."

The Bojo's head tilted a fraction as he looked directly at Katie for the first time. "And your guardian will attest to this?"

"He's not my guardian," Katie said, scowling. "And no. I snuck out. But I was here. All night."

"Making love in a child's bed?" asked the Bojo boss. His glassy gaze turned back to Sexton. "Why there?"

Sexton cleared his throat. "Well, because…"

"It's me," Katie interjected. "People died in the big bed. He found them there when he moved in. I refuse to use it. The thought of it just gives me the heebies."

She shuddered for effect, but didn't overdo it.

She was good, Sexton thought.

The Bojo boss's blade bumped lightly against his knee while he considered this.

Tap. Tap. Tap.

With a sharp nod, he rose, springing to his feet with an urgency that made Sexton's muscles tense in anticipation of a fight.

Once on his feet, though, the leader tucked his hands behind his back, along with the machete. "It appears we owe you chaps an apology," he said.

Sexton waved a hand. "It's fine."

"You're damn right you do!" Katie snapped. "But what about the door? And the furniture? Who's going to replace those?"

The other Bojos kept staring at the couple on the couch, but the boss's head turned as he took in the room, and the damage they had caused.

When he replied, his voice was questioning, with a hint of incredulity woven through it. "Well… you are," he said.

His tone darkened. "Or do you think we should be doing it, my dear?"

Katie's anger subsided. She clasped her hands in her lap and looked down. "Well, I mean… No. Obviously, we'll do it."

The flat side of the boss's blade pressed against her chin, forcing her head up until she could see herself reflected in his lenses. "See that you do," he instructed. "This place is a pigsty."

He lowered the blade, tucked it behind his back again, then gave both occupants of the couch a curt nod. "Best of British."

"Best of British," they both replied.

Sexton and Katie both remained seated until the Bojos had filed out, then hurried to close the door behind them. The wooden board had been torn away and tossed into the street, and most of the doorframe had splintered, so locking it was impossible.

The chain hadn't been on when they'd burst in, though, so Sexton used that to fasten the door closed as best he could, then caught Katie's arm before she could head up the stairs.

"Not yet. Give it a minute," he whispered, steering her back to the living room. "They might come back."

They stood just inside the doorway, ears open, voices low. Sexton shook his head, still not quite believing that they'd managed to get away with it. "They didn't find her. Why didn't they find her?"

"They didn't check under the bed. Because, you know, what kind of freaks would have sex on a bed with a kid hiding below it?" said Katie.

"Uh… we did," Sexton pointed out.

Katie snorted. "Please. We didn't have sex. You'd know if we'd had sex." She winked. "Trust me."

She motioned towards the hallway. "That's long enough. You wait by the door, I'll go upstairs and check on…" She mouthed an almost-silent, "You know who."

Sexton nodded his agreement, then went back to studying the door frame. Fixing it wasn't going to be easy.

Katie squeaked to the third step, then stopped. "You know you can't stay here. Right? Not now."

Sexton poked at the splintered wood for a moment, then ran his hand across the gloss of the door. It felt comforting. Familiar.

Home.

"Yeah," he said. His hand fell to his side, leaving a fading imprint of his fingers on the shiny surface. "I know."

Chapter 8

Marta was shaky, breathless, but mostly unharmed when Katie eventually brought her down the stairs. Nothing a couple of puffs on the inhaler couldn't fix. And possibly some therapy somewhere along the road.

Sexton was reluctantly forced to admit that, yes, they had to head for the border, and that, yes, Katie could be useful to bring along. That second part had taken some serious persuasion, although he couldn't deny that Katie had probably saved both him and Marta with her quick thinking.

The memory of her grinding naked on top of him didn't hurt, either, although he had made a noble attempt to not let that sway him.

He stood at the front door with Katie. He'd unfastened the chain, but kept his foot jammed against the door, holding it shut. He was confident the Bojos weren't waiting outside, but had sent Marta to hide in the bathroom, just in case.

"OK, so we have a plan," Katie whispered. "I'll go pick up some supplies, you pack what you can take from here, then I'll come back and we'll head out during the Reckoning when everyone's distracted."

Sexton winced, his fingers twitching into fists. Katie put a hand on his chest. "You can't. Even if you own up, they'll go ahead with it. They always do. It won't change anything."

"It's my fault," Sexton grunted.

"No. It's *their* fault. Those masked fuckers," Katie reasoned. "She's *Polish*, Rupert. You know what they'd have done to her."

Sexton nodded. He did. Not all of it, of course. But enough to have killed seven men on a beach to stop it happening.

He had no regrets about killing them. It was the consequences of that that he was going to have a hard time living with.

Katie prodded him, snapping him back to the present. "So, we go during the Reckoning. Right?"

Sexton nodded. "Right."

"Right."

She raised onto her tiptoes and kissed him on the cheek. From the way her eyes widened and her pale skin flushed red, this surprised her as much as it did him. She tucked a strand of her short hair back over her ear, stole a glance up the stairs, then gestured to the door.

"OK. Do it."

"Good luck," Sexton whispered. He removed his foot and pulled open the door. A weak late-winter sunlight flooded the hall, making them both screw their eyes shut and blink in its glare.

Katie screwed her eyes shut for a moment, then vanished between Sexton's blinks. There one moment, gone the next.

He looked out onto the street and saw her darting

along the empty pavement in the direction of the shop. To his relief, there was no sign of the Bojos.

Sexton took a moment to savour the fresh air of the outside world. *British air*, *the best bloody air in the world*, according to some. He didn't notice a lot of difference, himself, although it certainly smelled better now that the fires had mostly stopped springing up.

And, of course, once Brexit had closed all the factories, there was less pollution being spewed into the atmosphere. Still, he didn't think the air's 'Britishness' contributed anything to it.

Not that he'd ever say that out loud.

He retrieved the plywood board from where the Bojos had tossed it, stepped back into the house, and leaned the wood in place over the doorway. It wouldn't hold, but he didn't really need it to. It was just to keep up appearances for the next few hours.

That done, Sexton fastened the chain in place, wedged a piece of broken coffee table tightly under the bottom of the door, then creaked quickly up the stairs.

"Hey. It's me. It's Rupert," he said at the bathroom door.

There was some fumbling from the other side, then the lock disengaged, and the door opened just a crack. Marta peered out at him through the gap, her face a mess of tears and snot. She clutched a toothbrush like a weapon, her knuckles white on the handle.

It was, Sexton thought, one of the most heart-breaking things he'd ever seen. He knew, in that moment, that he was getting this girl to safety. No matter what it took.

"It's OK. You're OK," he assured her. He smiled. It wasn't an expression he had been familiar with for a while, so it felt a little unnatural. It seemed to do the trick, though, because Marta managed one of her own.

It was even less convincing than Sexton's, but it was a start.

"Everything's going to be fine. I promise," he told her, and the door opened a little more. "We're going to get you home."

———

"WHERE THE *FACK* HAVE YOU BEEN?" Nigel demanded when Katie entered strolled in through the front door, hands in the pockets of her thin jacket.

She looked across the counter at him in surprise. "Out. I told you, I was going for a walk."

"For an hour and a bleedin' half?"

Katie lifted the hatch and came behind the counter. "Well, *sorry*," she scowled. "I didn't realise I was up against the clock."

The back of his hand came out of nowhere, clipping her across the cheek. "You watch your fackin' mouth."

"Jesus! What the fuck?" she protested, but then shrunk back when he raised his hand again, making a fist this time.

"As long as you're under my roof, you'll show me some fackin' respect," Nigel warned. "Alright?"

He lunged a half-step towards her. "Alright?"

"Fine. Jesus. I'm sorry, OK? I won't take so long next time."

"See that you fackin' don't," he said. Catching her arm, he manhandled her into the back shop. "Now get through there and get to work. Them wank mags ain't going to organise them-fackin'-selves."

He lifted the hatch, stepped through, then lowered it again behind him. "And keep your eye on the shop for a while."

Katie leaned out from through the back. "Why? Where are you going?"

"None of your fackin' business. Out. That's where, alright?" Nigel spat at her.

"OK, well don't be long," said Katie, defiantly. She tapped her wrist where a watch might once have been. "Clock's ticking."

———

THE WORST THING about the Reckonings…

No. Wait. That was ridiculous.

One of the many terrible things about the Reckonings were that you didn't know where or when it was going to happen. Sure, you knew it was likely to be at some point on the day it was announced, but the Bojos never said exactly when it would be.

Afternoon was usually a good bet, but sometimes they were held late at night, too, the burning torches adding a certain dramatic ambience to proceedings.

Sexton had corralled Marta in the middle bedroom for the past hour, getting her to try on clothes while he'd packed some necessities of his own in his rucksack. He'd found an old *My Little Pony* school bag at the back of the cupboard in the hall, but it wasn't very big, and would be unlikely to hold much.

Mind you, Marta didn't look like she'd be able to carry it, if it had. There wasn't a lot of her, and the oversized clothes of the girl who'd once lived here practically drowned her.

As Sexton looked Marta up and down, Scotland suddenly seemed like a very long way away. He tried not to show his concern and gave her a thumbs up.

"Looking good," he told her. He looked to the radiator,

where he'd hung her own clothes during the night. It didn't work, of course, but he hadn't wanted to risk hanging them outside to dry, and not just because of the high likelihood of rain.

The bare white metal of the radiator gleamed back at him.

Huh. He was sure he'd left them there.

"Your clothes," Sexton said, pointing to the radiator. He ran a finger over it, finding moisture there. "Did you pack your clothes?"

Marta looked to the radiator. She looked up at Sexton. Her expression told him she didn't have the faintest idea what he was talking about.

"Shit," Sexton cursed. He searched the room, then raced through to the bathroom, hoping to find them there.

Nothing.

Oh, God.

Marta's clothes weren't in his bedroom. He tore through the rooms downstairs, hoping to find them sitting in a pile somewhere.

But no.

Oh, *fuck*.

They knew.

"We have to go," he told her. "It's not safe."

The tone of his voice frightened her. She retreated into herself, becoming smaller before his eyes. There was no time for reassuring words or comforting smiles, though. Not now.

They knew.

They fucking knew.

Swinging his rucksack onto his back, Sexton picked up the *My Little Pony* bag, bundled some clothes inside, then thrust it into Marta's arms. She caught it instinctively, then stared down at it like it was an unexploded bomb.

In the hall, he grabbed his own jacket from the hook, then rummaged among the others until he found one that must've belonged to the girl who used to live here. As with the rest of the clothes, it was too big, but it would have to do.

He wasted a second pulling his own jacket on, then several others helping Marta into hers. The sleeves hung down almost to her knees, while the drawstring hem at the bottom stopped just a few inches higher.

Sexton pulled Marta's hood up, but she almost got lost inside it, so he pushed it down again. "OK, bag on," he told her, holding the straps apart so she could manoeuvre her cumbersome arms through.

Once she was all zipped up and had the bag securely on her back, he took her by the arm and led her towards the door. He daren't risk going for Katie. Not in broad daylight. He'd get Marta out of town and they'd hide somewhere until nightfall, then – if possible – he'd come back for Katie.

But that was a big 'if.'

"Stay close to me and don't speak," he told Marta. He mimed drawing a zip across his lips, and she did the same. He hoped that meant she understood. Guess he'd find out.

The chain was still in place across the door. It was the only thing that prevented it falling open. He peered through the gap and saw that the board was still in place. He wished now that he hadn't replaced it, as it completely blocked his view of the street.

"Wait," he whispered, with an accompanying hand signal. He quietly unhooked the chain and eased the door open. Taking his knife in his hand, he inched the board out from the frame a fraction.

The grey March sunlight ebbed in. He saw a strip of

the cherry blossom tree, and part of the street beyond, but not much else. Nothing moved.

He listened but heard only the sounds of his own body – the thumping of his heart and the whooshing of blood through his veins.

Gripping the edge of the board, he dragged it aside, letting more light spill in. As the board was removed, it revealed a figure standing on the other side. Eyes glared out from the goggles it wore, partially obscured by the straw-like strands of the white blonde wig perched on top of the leather gasmask.

"Going somewhere, old boy?" asked the Bojo.

The board was wrenched from Sexton's grip. He hissed as one of the rusted nails tore across his palm, but the pain was quickly forgotten when the wood was tossed aside to reveal a whole gang of mask-wearing men in suits.

They each held weapons. Extending batons this time, rather than knives.

Small mercies.

"Marta, run!" Sexton warned, driving a kick into the stomach of the Bojo in the wig. He thrust with the knife, but a baton *cracked* him across the forearm, and the blade went clattering across the pavement.

He took the baton from the bastard as painfully as possible, then reintroduced him to it by cracking it across the side of his head. Once. Twice. The guy went down, but something exploded against Sexton's temple and the ground turned to quicksand beneath him.

He brought the baton up, blocking a potentially killer-blow, but – BAM! – a baton found his exposed ribcage, and pain flared through him, forcing him to his knees.

A hand caught him by the hair. He tried to stand, but suddenly the pavement was coming up, and it was all he could to do throw his hands in front of his face before he smashed against the paving slabs.

A toe of a boot found his already damaged ribs. The sole of another pressed on the back of his head, pressing his nose and forehead into the rough stone.

His ears were filled by the sounds of his skull creaking, and the muffled grunts of whoever's turn it was to kick him. He heard a voice, too. Familiar.

"See? I fackin' told you, didn't I? I told you!"

Nigel.

Over it all, Sexton heard the high-pitched complaining of the staircase as heavy feet rushed up it, giving chase.

No.

Sexton twisted, trying to heave himself out from beneath the boot. It pressed down harder. Something hammered into his lower back. A knee pressed down on his thigh from behind, the pain forcing a hiss from his lips.

His hands were wrenched behind him. Plastic ties dug into his wrists.

From inside the house there came a crash and the sound of a man screaming and screaming and *screaming*.

From the kitchen, Sexton thought. He snorted in something not unlike amusement, but then he heard another scream.

Marta.

The boot was removed. Sexton raised his head just as a baton swung down.

The impact jolted through his whole body. The pain erupted like a bomb.

And the world slipped away into a cool, inky darkness.

Chapter 9

Sexton awoke, slowly at first, then all of a sudden.

He jerked forward, but his restraints tightened, pulling him back onto the padded vinyl chair.

The sun was shining directly in his eyes, a fiery circle of blinding brilliance that…

Wait. No. Not the sun.

It was a light. An electric light. Jesus, he hadn't seen one of those in a while. Not operational, anyway.

His skull throbbed – a regular stabbing ache that pushed down on his head, forcing him deeper into the chair. He drew in a breath, which sent a crescendo of pain crashing through his bruised, battered, and very probably broken ribs.

The rest of the room was encased in shadow, the spotlight painting the rest of the room in dim silhouette. Sexton twisted his wrists together, and grimaced as the rope burned his skin.

His forearm caught on the back of the chair and pain pricked at him. Twisting his head, he saw a hospital drip-stand positioned off to the right of the chair, a bag of clear liquid hanging from it. A long thin tube trailed from the bottom of the bag, then disappeared behind him. He shook his arms as much as he was able to, and the tube jiggled around in time with the movements.

Shit. What now?

"Oh!" chimed a voice from the darkness. There was a giggle that made Sexton's skin crawl. "Look who's back in the land of the living."

A figure in a white apron appeared at the edges of the pool of light. Like the Bojos, he wore a mask, although this one was of the surgical variety, and only covered the bottom half of his face. Above them, he wore a set of brass-coloured goggles with mirrored lenses, and Sexton could see himself reflected in them both.

Christ, he was a mess.

Around each lens was a cog-shaped dial. They *clicked* softly as the wearer adjusted them. The lenses extended half an inch or so, and Sexton's reflections became warped and distorted.

"Where am I?" Sexton growled. His voice was like sandpaper on broken glass, each syllable thundering like a drumbeat inside his skull. "Where's the girl?"

"Wouldn't you like to know?" sniggered the man in the surgical mask. He tapped a rubber-gloved finger on the end of Sexton's nose. "*Boop*! Nosy Parker."

He leaned back and was swallowed by the darkness again. A zip was undone on Sexton's left a moment later, then was followed by the rustle of old leather.

"I am the Surgeon. That is what others refer to me as, at least. You should feel free to do the same."

His accent wasn't the same 'bumbling upper class oaf' that the Bojos aimed for. It still had that whiff of old money and in-breeding about it, but it sounded more natural, and less like the act the others put on. This guy was a proper toff. One of the real ones.

Fuck.

"They are too kind. Technically, I am but one of a number of surgeons. But, what can I say?"

He leaned into the light again. "They consider me the best."

He vanished once more, leaving just his creepy little snigger hanging in the air where he'd been.

From the darkness there came the *squeak* of rusty metal. A trolley was wheeled into view, a black leather bag sitting atop it.

The Surgeon stood right at the very edge of the darkness, the shadows feathering the bottom of his pristinely white apron. There was a *snap* of latex as he adjusted the gloves on his hands. Sexton watched the Surgeon's hand in the reflection of the goggles as it reached into the dark cavern of the bag.

"You have been a naughty boy, Mr. Sexton," the Surgeon said.

He withdrew a scalpel from the bag and placed it on the trolley.

Click.

"A very naughty boy. And do you know what we do to naughty boys here at the NHS?" He leaned in closer, his voice becoming a barely contained giggle of excitement. "Anything we want."

Sexton tried not to show his fear. He had suspected, of course, that he'd been handed over to the NHS, but he'd been silently praying that he was wrong.

The National Hurt Service – or National *Hunt* Service, depending on who you asked – had taken over all the abandoned hospitals and GP surgeries following the total collapse of the UK's health service.

The all-new NHS wasn't specifically loyal to any of England's Governors or Overlords but existed instead as a cross-territory service built on the founding principle of pain, torture, and violent dismemberment for all. Although Jeremy Hunt was no longer the UK Health Secretary back when everything went to shit, it was rumoured that he had been behind the original NHS's rapid post-Brexit decline, and the swift, bloody rise of its replacement.

"Where is the girl?" Sexton demanded. "What did they do with her?"

The Surgeon reached into the bag. He produced something that looked like a crochet hook, then set it down beside the scalpel.

Click.

"I'm afraid I wouldn't know," he said. There was that snigger again, like a public-school schoolboy getting up to mischief. He made a flourished gesture with his hand, like a magician drawing attention to his props. "Although, I am quite certain she's not a million miles away."

"Then she's alive?"

"For now," the Surgeon said. "Although, she may soon wish that she weren't."

The hand went back into the bag. A corkscrew was removed. The Surgeon held it up, studying it. He tutted softly, before flicking a piece of fluff off the end of the twisting metal spike.

Click.

It joined the other implements on the trolley. Sexton squirmed and heaved on his ropes, earning him a reproachful finger-wag from the man in the mask.

"Now, now, Mr. Sexton. Let's not make this any more difficult than it needs to be. Hmm?"

Sexton struggled for a second or two longer, then gave up with a sigh. His head swam from the effort.

"How long was I out?"

"Not long. An hour, perhaps. You're quite resilient. I am really rather impressed."

He fumbled in the bag again, before producing a small set of pliers.

"I do so enjoy a challenge."

Sexton regarded the growing assortment of tools and gave a few more frantic tugs on his ropes. The Surgeon's gloved hand rested on his shoulder, pushing him down into the seat.

"Shh, now, Mr. Sexton. Let's not get ourselves worked up. You'll disturb our other guest, and we don't want that." The Surgeon smirked behind his mask. "At least, not yet. She'll hear your screams eventually, of course. Who knows, if you hold out long enough, you may even get to hear hers."

"What about the Reckoning? Did they call it off?" Sexton asked.

"Ha!" said the Surgeon. "Of course not. It should be going ahead…" He fished in his apron pocket and produced a watch on a chain. "Oh! Within the hour. How exciting.

He slipped the watch back into his pocket. "It's a shame we won't get to attend, but then we'll be well underway by then, and so rather pre-occupied, I'm afraid."

"But they caught us. They found me. They don't need to punish anyone else," Sexton protested.

"Well, no. They don't *need* to do anything," the Surgeon agreed. "But wouldn't life be frightfully dull if we only ever did those things we *needed* to do? They'll hold the Reckoning because they can. Because it helps remind people just who is in charge."

He placed the back of a gloved hand to the side of his mouth, as if letting Sexton in on a secret. "And because a little birdie tells me they're going to have a rather special guest coming along to watch."

"Who?" Sexton asked.

"Oh, I couldn't possibly say," the Surgeon replied. He brought a long metal skewer from the bag and tapped a finger on the point, checking its sharpness. From the way he yanked the finger away again, it easily passed the pointiness test.

"You don't know, do you?" said Sexton. "They haven't told you."

"Nice try, Mr. Sexton. Of course they've told me," the Surgeon said. "But I, in turn, am electing *not* to tell you. I'm sure you understand. If it's any consolation, I hear they're only Reckoning a single individual this time," he continued, sounding almost disgusted by this. "They must be going soft."

Sexton nodded slowly. That was something. He flicked his eyes to the implements on the trolley just as the metal skewer was set down at a perpendicular angle below them, visually underlining the horrors that were about to unfold.

"Your file makes for interesting reading," the Surgeon said. He brought a small leather case from inside the satchel and unfastened the brass stud that held it together. The case spread apart like a butterfly's wings, revealing an assortment of drill bits on one side, and three hypodermic needles on the other.

"My file?"

"Don't look so surprised, Mr. Sexton. The NHS has files on everybody. But we're bound strictly by patient confidentiality, so the Bojos don't know who you are." He waggled his eyebrows. "Your secrets are safe with me."

"Then you know this isn't my first time in a chair like this one," Sexton said.

"Far from it, it seems. I am excited to discover what that could mean for our session."

Sexton indicated the tools with a nod of his head. "I'm not going to talk. You know that, right? Whatever you do, I'm not going to talk."

The Surgeon closed the zipper on his bag. "I don't want you to," he said with a shrug of his slender shoulders. "That's not why you're here. This isn't an interrogation, Mr. Sexton."

"Actually," said Sexton. "That's exactly what it was. I'm in the hospital. The girl's alive here, too. Alive. The Reckoning hasn't happened yet, and the Bojos don't know who I am. Oh, and they've got a special guest coming, but I couldn't really give a shit about that."

Sexton clicked his tongue against the back of his teeth, then nodded. "Yeah. I think that's everything."

He lunged, bringing both arms around behind him, one hand trailing a rope from the wrist. He had the scalpel before the Surgeon could react.

There was a *thwip*.

There was a gargle.

Red painted the top of the Surgeon's apron. Staggering back, he clamped a hand over the wound in his throat, desperately trying to stem the flow of blood that came pulsing between his fingers.

Sexton stood and untied the other end of the rope from his wrist, then watched, impassively, as the Surgeon fell to the floor. He walked slowly behind his would-be torturer as he tried to crawl to the door, leaving a slug-trail of crimson on the scuffed and faded linoleum.

The Surgeon's strength left him with a couple of feet to go. He wheezed and choked, his breath bubbling through the widening gash in his neck.

Sexton waited until the gasping had stopped, then

returned to the trolley. He selected the metal spike, and slipped it below his belt at the side of his hip. Then he took the corkscrew, positioning it in such a way that the curly spike protruded from between the middle and ring fingers of his left hand.

With his foot, he rolled the Surgeon onto his back, then fished the watch from his pocket. The time was a little after two-fifteen. The Surgeon had said the Reckoning was due to start in an hour. Say three o'clock to be on the safe side.

Forty-five minutes.

It was going to be tight.

Sexton angled the spotlight towards the door, then wheeled the trolley over to the door's right. He kicked it hard, sending it crashing across the room, where it smashed into a glass-fronted cabinet, shattering the glass.

The reaction from outside was instantaneous. The door unlocked with a *clunk* and an orderly in drab grey scrubs rushed in. He hissed in the glare of the light and threw up his hand to shield his eyes.

He managed to eject a single syllable of confusion, then the corkscrew punctured deep into his temple and his eyes rolled back in his head.

Sexton caught the man as he fell, carefully steering him away from the pool of blood as he set him on the floor. He was a big guy. About Sexton's size, in fact.

"Well, would you look at that," Sexton muttered, undoing the ties that held the orderly's scrubs in place. "Must be my lucky day."

Chapter 10

Marta lay on a hospital bed, straps fastening her arms and legs to the metal frame. There were five other beds around her. Four were empty. The fifth contained a man-sized lump that had been covered by a grimy white sheet. Blood stained the fabric roughly where the person's face would be.

A lot of blood.

There were no lights on the ward, aside from a single bare bulb that hung down from the ceiling on a length of wire. It flickered sporadically, and Marta gasped each time the room was plunged into darkness, fearing the light might never return.

Music played from an old battery-operated radio on the sill of the boarded-up window. A crackly version of Judy Garland's 'Get Happy' hissed out through the tinny speaker, urging Marta to forget her worries and chase all her cares away. Marta didn't understand the words, let alone appreciate their irony, and yet the song helped contribute to her overall mind-bending levels of terror.

She tried to cry out, but fear had formed a bubble in

her throat that prevented anything but the faintest of squeaks escaping.

The cold prickled her skin, making her flesh goose-bump and the hairs on her arms stand on end. It washed over her in regular waves, like the breathing of some ancient ice giant.

She tried to remember how she'd got here, but found nothing but fuzziness and a general sense of dread where the memory should have been.

Her sleeves had been rolled up. A brown sticking plaster had been applied to the crook of her right arm. There was something in her left hand. She craned her neck to look.

It was a lollipop.

Someone had placed a sticker on her chest. The text on it read: *The Doctor says, 'Well Done!'*

Marta couldn't understand the words. She had no idea why she was wearing it, or where it had come from.

The crackling voice on the radio churned out another of the song's repetitive verses.

Sing Hallelujah, come on get happy, it insisted.
Get ready for the Judgement Day.

———

SEXTON TWISTED the doctor's neck until it *cracked*, waited for the twitching to stop, then deposited him in the closest available storage closet. He had taken Sexton by surprise, stepping out of an office with a steaming hot cup of coffee in one hand, and a Polaroid camera in the other.

At first, the doctor had thought nothing of the man in the orderly's outfit, but when he'd done a double-take and a flicker of doubt had flitted across his features, Sexton took the executive decision to snap his neck.

For a hospital, the standard of cleanliness left a lot to be desired. Wheelchairs and gurneys lay abandoned and overturned in the corridors. Graffiti was daubed on the walls in a variety of viscous substances, none of them paint.

Bloodied bandages and dirty rags lay scattered across the floor. Paint peeled from the walls. Neon strip lights *buzzed* noisily overhead, painting the corridor in a glow that was almost certainly the most sterile thing in the place.

Of the seven rooms Sexton had checked in so far, two of them had been used as a toilet. Neither one had been designed for the purpose.

The end of this corridor had been adorned with a tattered George Cross flag. Someone had made an attempt at painting a swastika on the wall below it. It would've been more impressive had all four of the symbol's feet been pointing in the same direction.

Glass crunched beneath Sexton's feet as he crept on through the medical debris. The next room was empty, and – mercifully – devoid of human waste. The one after was a storage closet that reeked of death and decay. There was a bundle of sheets all piled up on the floor. Sexton chose not to investigate further.

It was no good. The hospital was a big place, and he didn't have a lot of time. He was starting to regret killing that doctor without asking for directions first.

There was nothing else for it. Sexton cupped his hands around his mouth and roared.

"Marta!"

His voice echoed off in both directions along the corridor, fading as it rolled away from him.

A door was pulled open up ahead. Two men in similar scrubs to his own came crashing out. They were big lads.

Brighter than they looked. They recognized him as an interloper at once.

"What's your fucking game?" one of the men demanded. He was the bigger of the two. Sexton went for him first, closing the gap between them with a brisk march, then driving the corkscrew into his throat with a well-aimed uppercut.

A mist of blood hit the other man's face, forcing him to blink through the spray. Sexton was on him before the first guy had hit the floor, slamming him against the wall and driving a flurry of crunching blows into his stomach and ribs.

"Where is she?" Sexton growled. The orderly tried to swing with a punch, but Sexton deflected it easily, then punished the guy with a headbutt that turned his nose into a grisly paste, and his legs into a wobbly jelly.

Bam! Sexton drove another punch into the orderly's stomach, drawing a wounded animal sob from his bloodied lips.

"Where is the girl?" Sexton demanded.

The orderly wheezed, his eyes wide with terror. "They'll k-kill me," he blubbered. "They'll kill me if I t-tell you."

Sexton dragged him to the floor, twisting his head until he was staring at the lifeless body of his companion, and the burbling blood oozing from his throat wound.

His voice was a menacing hiss in the orderly's ear.

"And what do you think I'm going to do to you if you don't?"

There was a *bang* from along the corridor, deafening in the enclosed space. Pain screamed across the top of Sexton's shoulder, and he felt a hot spray of blood cake the side of his neck.

Heaving the orderly up in front of him, he stumbled

for the open office door. The gunfire came again. The orderly jerked in his hands as two bullets punched through his chest and into the fleshy organs below.

Sexton let the guy drop and dived into the office, just as a fourth bullet ricocheted off the frame, splintering it. Slamming the door, he fumbled for the light switch and clicked it off. He leaped aside as another hail of bullets Swiss-cheesed the door, then pressed himself flat against the wall and waited.

The door *creaked* inward.

A hand slipped tentatively around the corner, searching for the light switch.

Sexton waited until it had found the switch, then buried the scalpel into the back of the hand, driving it all the way through the bone and into the plastic cover of the light switch.

He swung out, getting so up close and personal with the gunman that the gun was rendered more of a hindrance than a help. Sexton took the weapon from him, then sent him stumbling across the room with a twist and a shove. The man – another orderly – screamed as his hand ripped the scalpel free of the light switch, but stopped abruptly when his legs gave way and he crashed into a stack of metal bed pans.

"Fuck!"

Sexton glanced at the gun. Smith & Wesson. US-made, naturally. For all their hatred of foreigners, Brexiteers generally jizzed their loads over all things American. This was despite the fact that the 'special relationship' between the US and the UK had done nothing to mitigate the consequences of the no-deal Brexit.

Of course, for many of the more rabid Brexiteers, the country was exactly as they'd always wanted it to be.

After checking the gun over and peering along its

sights, Sexton shot the orderly in the leg, just above the knee. The man opened his mouth to scream, but Sexton wedged the muzzle of the gun between his teeth, forcing the cry back down into his throat.

The guy was young. Early-twenties. Young enough to still have acne. Stupid enough to have tried to bury it beneath several tattoos so bad he might very well have done them himself.

He gagged and choked on the gun's barrel. The floor beneath him prevented him from pulling his head away, and tears streamed down his face as he was forced to deep throat the warm metal.

"Where is she?" Sexton asked.

The orderly tried to speak, but it came out as a string of unintelligible sobs and gargles.

"I'm going to ask you again," Sexton told him. "Where is the girl? I would advise you to not waste my time."

The orderly gasped and grunted in response, then retched violently as the end of the weapon pressed deeper into his throat.

"Three," said Sexton.

The orderly wailed on the end of the gun.

"Two."

Sexton placed a hand in front of the man's face, ready to block the blood, bone and brain matter that was about to come exploding towards him.

"One."

"NEEEEEEUUURRMF!" squealed the orderly, flopping around on the floor in panic.

Sexton withdrew the gun from the man's mouth and jammed it against his forehead, instead. "Do I have your attention?" he asked.

"Yes. Y-yes!"

"Good. Now, I'm going to count down from three

again, and if you don't tell me where the girl is before I get to one, I'm going to put a hole in your face."

He drew back the slide, chambering a round.

"Now, if you're ready," he said. "Then, we'll begin."

———

MARTA DIDN'T KNOW what the men were saying, but it was clear they were all angry about something. They barked orders at one another, each of them biting back at the other three, flashing their fists and their teeth and the weapons they carried.

Two of them clutched long knives. The third and fourth wielded a cricket bat and shotgun respectively. The bat had several long nails driven through the wood, and the bald-headed man holding it looked like he'd get a real kick out of using it.

None of them wore full-face masks like the other men she'd seen had. Instead, they had white paper masks across their mouths, like they were worried about catching a disease of some kind.

Marta stayed as quiet as she could. They knew she was there, of course. They loomed in a semi-circle around her bed, occasionally gesturing to her as they argued. If she stayed quiet, she thought, maybe they wouldn't hurt her. Maybe they'd let her go.

She glanced from their twisted-up faces to their weapons again.

There was no way they were letting her go.

The lights flickered. The radio, which had been crackling out that same up-tempo song on a loop ever since she'd woken up, sputtered into silence for a moment, then returned as nothing but static.

One of the men with the knives stormed over to the

radio and clicked it off. The lightbulb flickered again, and Marta caught just the briefest glimpse of something pouncing on the man from the shadows before the darkness settled across the room.

The thing that had pounced on the man had seemed monstrous, almost completely awash with blood. The way it leaped on him was savage and animal-like. He barely had time to eject the start of a yelp before he was silenced.

The other men turned in the direction of the sound. They spoke in urgent tones, then jumped in fright as the light returned for a split-second, revealing the blood-soaked figure looming ahead of them.

The man with the gun fired, a booming roar that lit-up the empty space where the figure had been, and made Marta cry out in fright.

There was a lot of shouting after that, mostly from the other two men. They reacted angrily to the gunshot, and only stopped when the gun itself clattered to the floor.

From the darkness came a wet, bloody gargle, then the soft *thump* of a body crumpling to the floor. The shouting took on a more panicky edge. The light returned in a series of staccato flashes.

Three men stood in a line, a body on the floor between them. The man with the cricket bat swung, just as the darkness returned. Marta heard the low *whum* of it swishing through the air, then the sickening crunch of a nail being driven into bone.

Another burst of light pushed back the shadows, revealing just two men standing there, both wearing masks. The one closest to Marta dropped his knife and stumbled as blood seeped out through a hole in the side of his head.

He muttered something. Even if Marta had been able to speak English, she didn't think she'd have been able to understand it. It was more of a moan than anything that resembled actual words.

The man with the bat spun around in a panic, lashing out at thin air as his colleague crumpled to the ground. Marta saw the bat-wielder's head snap towards her, his eyes blazing. He began to move just as the darkness rushed back in.

A moment later, he was standing over her, the bat raised above his head. She saw it even in the gloom, held ready to swing down at her head. She struggled against her bonds as the man roared commands into the darkness. It was no use. The straps were too tight. Too strong. There was nothing she could do but lie there and wait for the—

The light returned. The man with the bat looked down at his feet, then vanished out of sight. He shouted the same word several times. It was one Marta knew.

"No, no, no, no, no—"

There was a commotion beneath Marta's bed. The shouting stopped. The light went out again.

When it returned, another man stood over the bed where the bat-wielder had been. Despite the blood that stained his green smock and covered his face, Marta wasn't afraid.

She managed a smile. It was small and shaky, but a smile all the same.

"Ru-pert," she said.

Sexton nodded down at the girl. She seemed unhurt. Shaken, obviously, but unharmed.

Lucky for them.

"It's OK, kid," he told her, unfastening the first of her straps. "Everything's going to be OK."

Chapter 11

Time was running out. Sexton wasn't crazy enough to think he could stop the Reckoning, but they could still use it as cover to get out of town.

There would still be road blocks, of course, but they could find a way past those. There weren't enough Bojos to guard every possible route out of town. Not by a long shot.

Getting out of the hospital had been easier than Sexton had expected. He'd been bracing himself for more orderlies to try to stop him, but either he'd already killed them all, or those who were left had seen sense.

Probably the former, he thought.

He checked a few rooms but couldn't find his rucksack or the *My Little Pony* bag anywhere. He had struck gold with a couple of inhalers, though, and had bundled those into his pockets along with a few half-empty boxes of antibiotics he'd found on the wards. There wasn't time to keep searching for the rest of their gear, though. They'd just have to find supplies on the road.

Sexton lurked just inside the hospital's sliding glass doors, peering out through the layer of grime that coated it. Although the hospital clearly had power, the sensor above the door had been disabled, and Sexton had to manually heave it open when he was sure the coast was clear.

He indicated for Marta to wait while he checked to make sure that no-one was lying in wait outside, then beckoned for her to follow. She raced to catch up, only slowing when she was close enough to grab for his hand.

Sexton looked down in surprise at the hand clutching the ends of his fingers. His own hand remained rigid, as if frozen solid.

Then, after a moment, it thawed. He adjusted his grip until her hand slipped fully into his.

Yes. He'd get her out of town. He'd get her to safety, even if it was the last thing he did. *Especially* if it was the last thing.

He was halfway through making a plan that involved following the coast out east when Marta said something that upped and ruined everything.

"Katie."

Sexton shook his head. "No. It's too dangerous. We can't go back."

Marta's mouth attempted a few different shapes, before settling on one. "Bad… men."

"Exactly. The bad men. We can't go back because of the bad men."

Marta looked confused. She tried again. "Bad… men. Katie."

Sexton stopped.

The clothes. They'd found Marta's clothes.

They knew Katie had lied to them.

They knew. The bad men knew.

'A single individual.' That's what the Surgeon had said. The Bojos were only Reckoning one person.

Shit.

Sexton tightened the grip on Marta's hand, shook his head, and marched on.

No. Not his problem.

He reminded himself that he was a bastard. Always had been. Always would be.

He stopped again.

"Fuck!" he spat, and Marta pulled her hand away in fright. He stood there on the cracked tarmac of the hospital drop-off, his lips moving silently as he plotted.

Turning, he took in the immediate surroundings. The hospital car park was a graveyard of abandoned vehicles. The bus stop across the road was a tangle of metal and broken glass, something heavy having ploughed through it at some point in the not-too-distant past.

More cars had been abandoned on both sides of the road that ran along the front of the hospital. Something heavy had passed between them, tearing the metal and scraping the paintwork down their sides, and shoving them all against the kerb.

The path of cleared vehicles led almost all the way up to where Sexton stood. Frowning, he turned and projected the trail suggested by the damage. It ran right along the front of the hospital towards the 'No Parking' zone outside the A&E department entrance.

His breath snagged at the back of his throat when he saw what stood there. He stared at it for a while, a grim smile tugging at one corner of his mouth.

In his pocket, the Surgeon's watch ticked steadily on towards three o'clock.

"OK, Marta," he said. He held his hand out to her again. "Here's what we're going to do."

———

KATIE STUMBLED BLINDLY as a hand shoved her hard in the back. She yelped, the sound echoing strangely in the cloth bag that had been tied over her head. She tried to throw out her hands to find her balance, but the ropes were too tight, and all she could do was brace herself before her shoulder slammed into the ground and the crowd erupted in laughter and cheering.

Voices bellowed at her. Men, mostly, but there was the occasional female screech mixed in with it.

"Traitor!"

"Evil Remoaner bitch!"

"String her up, the fucking slag!"

A hand, the same one that had pushed her, she guessed, caught her by the arm and wrestled her violently to her feet.

"Move," urged a Bojo, snapping a punch against the back of her head that almost made her bite through her tongue. She staggered again, but this time the Bojo didn't let her fall.

Something pelted her on the chest, and she felt a cold wetness seep through her shirt.

"Ungrateful bitch!" roared a voice from somewhere so close up she blinked and drew back in fright.

"N-Nigel," Katie whimpered. "Help me. Don't let them do this."

"Why the *fack* should I help you, eh?" Nigel barked. He slapped her, his hand stinging her even through the bag. "Never should've taken you in in the fackin' first place. If your old man could see you now, he'd be ashamed."

She heard him spit up close in her face. At least the sack stopped her feeling that.

Over the angry shouts of the mob, Katie heard the *swishing* of the waves lapping up the beach. She focused on that, trying to ignore the shouted insults, hurled abuse, and the threats from the men who wanted her to know *exactly* what they'd do to her, given half a chance. *Dirty slut like her'd probably fackin' love it, too*, they cackled as she was huckled past them by the Bojo at her back.

The worst of it was, some of them might get the chance. She hoped that came after, at least, and not before.

Someone grabbed at her arse as she passed by. Another had a go at her tits, sniggering as he groped at them, only stopping when the Bojo marched her on.

She listened to the waves, imagining herself out there somewhere. Far away.

"Steps," said the voice in her ear, and she blindly raised a foot like some performing seal, which annoyed her immensely.

The first step *creaked* beneath her weight. Wooden.

So, they were hanging her, then. Made sense.

She wasn't moving quickly enough for the Bojo's liking. He shoved her on and she fell against the next few steps, cracking her shins against the sharp wooden edges.

"Get a move on, my dear," growled a voice from above her. Rough hands grabbed her by the back of the t-shirt and dragged her up the steps, exposing her back and most of her midriff to the jeering crowd.

"Get her fackin' tits out for the lads!" bellowed someone in the crowd.

"I've already had a peek, when she was passed-out pissed one night," came a laughing reply. Nigel, Katie realised. "They ain't up to much."

"Prick!" Katie cried, but a fist hit her in the mouth and she felt her lip split against her bottom teeth.

"Do shut up, won't you?" said a Bojo, so close that Katie could feel his breath through both his mask and hers. "There's a good girl."

She listened to the waves.

Ah, fuck it, she thought. *In for a penny…*

She snapped her head forward, connecting hard with the Bojo in front of her. He hissed in pain, and she barely had time to eject a satisfied little laugh before a left hook exploded against the side of her head.

"You dirty traitor slut!" the Bojo spat, grabbing her by the shirt.

The other man behind her intervened. "Not yet, old boy. You'll get your chance," he said. "Let's wait for our guest to turn up first, what?"

The hand twisted the fabric of her shirt, screwing it into a ball. She spat blood against the inside of her hood and braced herself for another strike.

It didn't come. Not yet, anyway. The hand released its grip.

"String her up," the man in front commanded, much to the delight of the gathered mob.

A rope was lowered and secured around her neck, then tightened just enough that she felt she was about to be lifted off her feet. Not enough to strangle her, just enough to partially cut-off her air supply and set her panicking.

The bag was pulled away. The crowd was revealed.

It was made up of two very distinct parts. The part of the audience closest to the platform where she stood was rabid and red-faced. She didn't see Nigel at first, because most of the other men there looked just like him. Hell, a few of the women, too.

Most of the other women in that part of the crowd were brash and blonde, with make-up applied in generous layers on top of fake-tan. They snarled up at her, screeching and cackling like witches, their painted faces all shrivelled with hatred.

This part of the crowd was a sea of Union Flags and George Crosses that fluttered proudly in the breeze blowing in off the Channel. There were a few home-made signs, too. They called for 'Death to All Traytors,' and demanded 'Foriners Out!'

Cretins.

The rest of the crowd hung back from the action along the Esplanade a little. They didn't shout or jeer or wave illiterate banners. They stood reluctantly at the fringes, flanked by Bojos. They weren't there because they wanted to be, but because they had no other choice. A Reckoning demanded attendance. There weren't a lot of laws left these days, but that was one of them.

The less-fervent group outnumbered the more dedicated one by two or three to one, but it was the feverish mob section that drew all the attention.

There had to be three or four hundred of them, all calling for her to be killed. And those were the friendlier ones. She tried not to listen to what the others wanted to do with her.

They wanted to scare her, she knew, and they were doing a fucking stellar job of it. Still, she wasn't going to let them see that.

"Just so everyone knows," she shouted. "I saw Nigel's dick, too, when he tried to stuff it in my mouth one night and I punched him in the balls. It's like a little worm."

"Shut the fack up, you lying slag!" Nigel barked.

"Seriously, it's like a child's penis. It's pathetic," Katie said.

She savoured the boos and jeers that followed, but enjoyed even more the way Nigel's cheeks burned with embarrassment.

A Bojo in a blonde wig stepped out in front of the wooden platform where Katie stood on display, and was greeted by enthusiastic applause from the mob. He basked in it for a moment, then held up his hand for silence.

It arrived immediately, everyone knowing better than to keep a Bojo waiting.

He stood there, unmoving, his hand raised, his eyes hidden behind the misty lenses of his mask until the waves themselves seemed to fall silent. Only then did he speak. His voice was soft and quiet, yet seemed to roll all the way from one end of the Esplanade to the other.

"Now, then. Which of you chaps is ready for a Reckoning?"

The mob erupted in another round of cheering. The Bojo tucked his thumbs into the lapels of his suit jacket and rocked back on his heels, and let the excitement continue for a while. He looked around and up at Katie, and she saw herself reflected in his lenses.

"Hang the bitch!"

"Teach her a fucking lesson!"

The Bojo held up his hands for silence again. The speed with which it fell was genuinely impressive, almost like some kind of magic trick.

"Of course, we can't just hang her without due process," the Bojo said. "This is England. We are a democracy."

He gestured up at Katie with a dramatic flourish. "All those in favour of the reckoning, say 'Aye!'"

The roar was deafening, though not unexpected. The Bojo mimed being pushed back by the force of it, drawing a laugh from the audience that was too loud and too long.

"All those against, say 'Nay!'" the Bojo urged.

Silence.

Well, almost.

"Nay," said Katie. "Big nay from me. *Hard* nay."

One of the two men with her on the platform struck her across the back of the legs with a baton, and she decided against protesting further.

"The 'Ayes' have it. The people have spoken," the Bojo boss bellowed. "A Day of Reckoning is upon this green and pleasant land."

The mob reached fever pitch. They punched the air and waved their little flags, practically frothing at their mouths with anticipation. This was probably the most excitement most of them had had since the Sun had dropped Page 3.

Still, Katie thought, at least they hadn't started singing *Jerusalem*, although it was probably only a matter of time. If they started with that shit, she'd jump her fucking self.

From her high vantage-point, Katie saw a long black car appear around the corner at the end of the Esplanade. It was flanked on both sides by several gun-toting Bojos. They all wore gasmasks and wigs, and jogged alongside the car as it cruised towards the crowd, keeping pace with it.

The sight of it so surprised her that she temporarily forgot her predicament.

"What the hell is this now?" she wondered.

Down in front, the Bojo leading the show continued with his speech. "This woman – this *traitor* – betrayed us all today, friend. Betrayed the very country to which she belongs. And how, you ask? I'll tell you."

He had been pacing before the crowd, but now stopped, stock-still. "She concealed the presence of a Johnny."

Gasps went up. Booing followed. The mob, which had hated her at that point because it had been told to, now hated her for what she had done.

"Yes! She concealed a filthy Johnny Foreigner, going so far as to aid in the murder of a squadron of fine, upstanding Englishmen whose only crime was a desire to keep our borders secure – to keep us safe – so that the interloper could go undetected."

"She's a little girl!" Katie protested, but the raging of the crowd drowned her out. She persevered, regardless. "And I didn't kill anyone!"

"This wasn't simply an attack on the Bojos," the boss-man continued. "It was an attack on all of us. It was an attack on the very soil of England itself! And such attacks simply will. Not. Stand!"

He rocked back on his heels again, letting the excitement build for a while. Just as it seemed like those at the front of the mob might be about to storm the gallows and hang Katie themselves, he gestured for silence.

"This is a very special Reckoning," he said, lowering his voice so those at the back had to strain to hear. "We have this treacherous creature to do with as we please. Her accomplice and the Johnny had been handed into the care of the NHS."

"Gawd bless it!" said a man near the front.

There was a worried silence for a few seconds as the mob waited to see how the Bojo would react, only easing when he responded with a nod. "God, as you say, bless it," the boss-man agreed. "The accomplice and the Johnny will both be discharged later today. What's left of them, anyway. They shall then be handed into the custody of a rather special guest."

Katie looked across the heads of the crowd. The black car was drawing level with the stragglers near the back. They jumped aside in surprise as it prowled through them, its engine whisper-quiet.

"He's come all the way from his stronghold in Plymouth to be here," the Bojo leader said. "I trust you shall all join me in showing our great respect, admiration, and appreciation for everything he has done."

An expectant hush descended as the car pulled up in front of the gallows. It had probably been a sleek, elegant-looking vehicle once, but the armour-plating affixed all over it had well and truly put a stop to that.

Several more armed Bojos appeared and formed a defensive barrier between the crowd and the car.

"Ladies. Englishmen," said the Bojo boss. "It gives me the greatest pleasure to introduce to you our very special guest. Our glorious lord and master…"

The car door opened. From Katie's angle, she couldn't see who emerged at first. Not until the shock of white-blonde hair appeared.

Not a wig this time. This was the real deal.

"Hol-ee shit," she whispered, barely able to believe her eyes.

It was him. It was actually him. He was actually here.

The Man Himself.

Boris.

Chapter 12

Katie had never seen Boris Johnson in the flesh before, and flesh was something he had in abundance. He had gained a good couple of stone since those TV interviews in the days surrounding the UK's disastrous exit from the EU. Wherever he was living, he wasn't surviving on Pot Noodles, that much was clear.

He waved almost regally to the assembled crowds, most of the members of which seemed to be in a state of shock. A few near the front were crying into their flags – hot, happy tears of hope and joy.

Others just stared in awe and wonder, mesmerised by the very sight of him, reeling that he was standing there before them, arms open and welcoming like some Eton-educated Christ.

"Hello there!" he called. "Jolly nice to see you all! Gosh! What a turnout!"

"We love you, Boris!" squealed a woman from the mob.

"How very kind of you to say so. I, in return, of course, am utterly infatuated with you all, too."

He clapped his hands once and rubbed them together. "Now, where's this ruffian who's caused all this trouble, hmm?"

One of the gun-toting Bojos leaned in and mumbled something. Boris jumped as if he'd been electrocuted, then turned and looked back over his shoulder. He smiled up at Katie, but his eyes betrayed him. They were cold and calculating, yet blazed with something wild and unpredictable. The eyes of a madman.

"Aha! There's the bounder." He shook a fist in Katie's direction. "Boo! Hiss! Grrr! And so on, and so forth. Down with that sort of thing!"

The audience laughed, egged-on by the Bojos. Boris patted the pockets of his suit trousers, as if searching for his car keys. "Right, then. So… what? We should probably get it underway."

"Speech!" urged a voice in the crowd. Another echoed it. And another. Soon, the mob were chorusing the word as if one voice.

"Speech! Speech! Speeeech!"

Boris ran his fingers through his unkempt locks and puffed out his cheeks. He looked sceptical for a moment, but then grinned cartoonishly out at the crowd. "Oh, go on, then. Just a small one. Don't say I'm not good to you."

He cleared his throat while he waited for the cheering to die down. When it started to drag on too long, he gave the nod to the Bojo-boss, who gestured for calm.

"Thanks awfully," said Boris, giving the man a second nod. He slipped one hand into a pocket, waved vaguely with the other, and began to talk. "To paraphrase some coloured chap or other, I have a dream. A dream of a strong, noble England, standing proudly on its own two feet, free of the shackles placed upon it by those rather rum chaps across the Channel."

There was a murmuring of agreement and a passionate, "Hear, hear," from the mob.

"An England that stands head and shoulders above the other countries on the world's stage, lighting the way that others may follow. From a distance, I mean," he assured the crowd. "We don't want the buggers coming over here now, do we?"

The consensus from the crowd was that no, they jolly well did not.

"An England where good, solid, dependable and hard-working English-born men and woman can thrive and prosper, working together to make this sceptred isle the very best it can be. Better. Faster. Stronger."

Up on the gallows, Katie snorted. "That's the Six Million Dollar Man."

Boris turned to her again, a look of buffoonish confusion on his broad face. "I'm sorry?"

"'Better, faster, stronger.' That's from the Six Million Dollar Man," Katie said. "The old TV series. With Wotsisname in it? Lee Majors. My dad used to make me watch it."

Boris blinked. "I'm sorry, I don't have the faintest idea what you're talking about. I was referring to England."

"How can England be 'faster'?" Katie asked. "It's not going anywhere."

"It's going straight to the top!" called one of the more delusional members of the audience.

"Bollocks," Katie scoffed. "Down the toilet, maybe."

"Shut the fack up, you slag!" barked someone in the crowd.

Boris nodded in agreement. "Yes. You heard the chap. Shut it, *you slag*." He gave another wave of his fist, then gestured to the Bojo standing at Katie's side. "Be a good fellow and give her a slap, would you?"

He did. Katie swore at him.

"Top man," said Boris. "Now, where was I?"

He *umm*ed and *aah*ed a few times as he tried to find his way back into his speech, then eventually managed to pick up the thread.

"I appreciate that things have not necessarily been easy. For any of us. I, myself, am currently embroiled in a war with the blasted Moggies out west, and there are pockets of Grovers springing up all over the place. I've spoken to Michael about that – gave him a jolly good ear-bashing, in fact – but he says one thing, then does another. Frightful little man."

Realising he was getting side-tracked, Boris moved to bring the speech home. "The point is, no matter how hard it may be at the moment, we should all take great comfort and solace in the knowledge that it shall get better. Not today, or tomorrow, perhaps. Or the next day, or necessarily the day after that, or the day after *that*. But, it shall get better. We persevere. We thrive. Together. Eventually."

Boris drew in a long breath and pointed emphatically to the ground at his feet. "And we do it for this blessed plot. This earth. This realm. This *England*."

The cheering completely drowned out the sound of the engine until it was too late. The first that most people knew about the arrival of the ambulance was when it ploughed into the back of the angry mob, turning their cheering and applause into screaming and chaos.

While it was still recognisable as an ambulance – the blue lights, yellow-and-green checks, and the word 'Ambulance' printed across the front were all giveaways – it had a number of notable additions.

The corrugated iron over the windows was one major part of the redesign. Slots had been cut in the metal, affording the driver a view of the road, albeit a pretty restricted one.

Razor wire ran along the sides of the vehicle and up onto the roof. More metal plating had been affixed over the wheel wells, presumably to stop anyone shooting out the tyres.

Arguably the most notable change – and certainly the one causing most concern among the mob – was the assortment of rusty metal spikes that had been affixed to the front bumper and grille, many of which were now buried deep in the flesh of screaming Brexiteers.

The screaming intensified when the gun-toting Bojos opened fire on the ambulance, cutting down a dozen people in the space of a few seconds.

Katie could only watch as the bullets tore through flesh, met metal, then ricocheted off. Just in front of her, one of the Bojos forcibly bundled Boris into his car, but the mob had started to throng past the vehicle in their panic, and there were too many of them to safely plough through.

"Get out of the way! Get out of the fucking way!" roared a Bojo, hacking and slashing with his machete. The Bojos up on the gallows jumped down to lend a hand. Katie couldn't look away as they set about stabbing and chopping anyone who was blocking the car's path.

"Moggies. It's the fucking Moggies!" cried one of the gunmen. He and the others all opened fire again, their bullets hammering into the armoured ambulance and sparking whenever they hit the metal plating.

The ambulance's engine was still running, but the carnage beneath its front wheels had stopped it going anywhere. One of the gun-Bojos approached the driver's door while the other covered him. Tentatively, he reached for the door handle and yanked it open, snapping his rifle up as he did.

"Empty," he hollered over the screeching crowd. He reached inside, and the engine spluttered into silence. When he appeared again, he was holding a brick in one hand. "It's empty. They propped the fucking accelerator pedal with—"

There was a bang. A bullet passed cleanly through the Bojo's chest and *whanged* off the side of the ambulance just a fraction of a second before the blood-spray painted the metal.

There was a confused silence for a split-second, before one of the Bojos spun and opened fire on the others. Heads exploded. Brains erupted. Pulp and goo and the whistle of hot bullets filled the air.

Katie watched with interest. This was an interesting development.

That one Bojo took out the others with remarkable efficiency, wasting not a single one of the five bullets he fired. Of course, now wasn't the time to go resting on his laurels.

"Look out!" Katie warned.

He turned, caught a glimpse of the machete-wielding Bojo behind him, then slammed the butt of the rifle into the guy's face. Protected only by a thin plastic mask, the knifeman's nose crumpled, ejecting blood through the die-cut nostrils.

Katie's heart leapt as the Bojo with the gun pulled of his gasmask and tossed it aside.

"Where the fuck did you come from?" she asked him. "I thought they took you to the hospital."

Sexton shrugged, then shot two more Bojos trying to flank him around the sides of the gallows.

"I discharged myself. You OK?" he asked.

Katie raised her bound-together hands and indicated the noose. "Had better days," she said. "Where's Marta?"

"Safe," said Sexton. "I'll get you down in— "

The armoured car slammed into him, bouncing him across the bonnet and onto the roof, before depositing him unceremoniously back onto the ground again. There was a series of *thuds* and *crunches* as Boris's car careened through a knot of fleeing spectators, scattering the lucky ones and dragging a less fortunate few beneath the wheels.

Spinning up onto a knee, Sexton peppered the back of the car with gunfire. Its tyres howled as the car weaved erratically along the Esplanade, skidded a good thirty feet, then smashed into a concrete bollard. The horn blared out a single continuous note, like a ship lost out at sea.

Sexton struggled to his feet, clutching his ribcage. He watched as the car's back door opened and Boris fell clumsily onto the tarmac. With a grunt, Sexton pulled himself onto the first step of the gallows, but a shout from Katie stopped him going any further.

"What the fuck are you doing?" she demanded. "He's one of the ones who caused all this. Fucking shoot him!"

Sexton blinked, as if making sense of what she'd said, then turned and raised the rifle just as Boris went stumbling into an alleyway between two boarded-up restaurants.

"Shit."

"Go after him," Katie urged. She brought her hands up and dug her fingers in below the noose around her neck. "I'll be fine. Don't you dare let that Tory fuck get away."

Sexton stole a glance around. Most of the Bojos were dead. The others were running, having completely lost control of the crowd. The people who hadn't wanted to be here in the first place no longer were, and the ugly mob of Brexiteers was thinning by the second.

Fuck it.

"I'll be right back," Sexton told her. He started to run, then hesitated. "You sure you'll be—"

"Go!"

With a nod, Sexton set off, KO'ing a tattooed skinhead who stupidly tried to block his path with a single blow from the butt of the gun. Pain turned his legs heavy, but he limped hurriedly on, gritting his teeth and ignoring the multitude of tiny searing agonies that jabbed at him.

This wasn't part of the plan, but Katie was right. It was too good an opportunity to miss. Johnson ruled the territory from Oxford all the way to Land's End. Go high enough up the chain, and the Bojos answered to him. He was behind every murder, every torture, every Day of Reckoning inflicted on innocent people over the past year.

Not to mention being responsible for the whole sorry mess in the first place, thanks to his lies and deception. Sometimes, when he closed his eyes, Sexton could still see that big red bus promising hundreds of millions a week for the NHS.

The real NHS, not the twisted mockery it had now become.

It was Boris's doing. Boris's fault.

And Sexton was going to make him pay.

Back at the gallows, Katie struggled against the noose. The problem was that the rope was pulled too tight. The way it dragged her onto her tiptoes made it virtually impossible for her to get enough leverage to slacken the rope off and pull herself free. The way the gallows shook as the final few stragglers all ran for safety wasn't helping, either.

"Come… on," she wheezed, straining to reach the noose's knot. It was behind her head, though, and having both hands tied together made it difficult to reach.

She had just got a fingertip to it when she heard the creaking of the steps.

Katie managed to turn enough to see the overweight balding figure heave himself onto the platform beside her.

"Well now, sweetheart," said Nigel, looking her up and down. His slug-like tongue emerged from within his mouth and flicked hungrily across his lips. "Seems to me like you've found yourself in a right old pickle."

Chapter 13

Sexton checked the car. The driver was dead, as evidenced by the way his face was hanging off, and the way the insides of his head painted the front windscreen. Lucky shot.

Turning away, Sexton hurried into the alleyway Boris had fled into. It was tight and narrow in there, rendering the rifle useless. He swung it on its strap over his shoulder and jogged on.

The alleyway opened into a network of back yards. The fences that had run between them had all been pulled down. They were probably barricading a window somewhere now, if they hadn't been used for firewood.

The ground was an expanse of badly laid tarmac, with oily puddles dotted around the uneven ground. Little circles *plinked* in the puddles as rain began to fall. It rattled on the metal lid of an old covered skip, almost covering the sound of movement from inside.

Almost.

Sexton approached the skip and used the barrel of the gun to push open one flap of the lid. The smell that rose from within was eye-watering, and forced him to clamp a hand over his nose and mouth before examining it any more closely.

There were a couple of bodies in there amongst the trash. From the condition of them, they weren't recent additions.

A couple of rats squirmed around in the corner, dazzled by the sudden light. Sexton lowered the lid again, muttered, "Shit," below his breath, then turned just in time for a length of metal pipe to *crack* him across the side of the head.

The world became weirdly two-dimensional for a moment as a flash of white obscured the vision in his left eye. The ground dragged him down. He tried to raise the gun, but there was nothing to shoot at but the rain.

BAM!

The pipe struck him across the back of the head and he face-planted into a greasy puddle. Pressing his hands flat against the ground, he tried to push himself back up, but a foot stamped down on him, driving him down into the water.

"There's a good chap. Stay right there," bumbled the owner of the foot.

Sexton groaned. He'd let himself get blindsided. Worse than that, he'd let himself get blindsided by Boris fucking Johnson. He was never going to live this down.

Assuming he lived at all.

The gun was taken from him. When he tried to take it back, the pipe smashed across his upper back, ejecting what little air he had left into the puddle as a series of grimy bubbles.

"Now, now. No grabbing. There's a good chap," Boris said. "Now, I wonder… How do I work this baby?"

The series of *clacks* that followed told Sexton he knew

full well how to work it. The rifle's barrel pressed against the back of Sexton's skull, forcing his face further into the water.

A kick to Sexton's ribs forced him to gasp. He coughed and spluttered in panic as the cold water flooded his nose and mouth, filling it with an acrid, coppery tang.

"Well, this is fun, isn't it?" Boris said. "But I'm afraid we're going to have to make an example of you."

———

NIGEL ADVANCED ACROSS THE PLATFORM, that horrible purple tongue still sliding its head out between his lips.

"Think you can embarrass me, do ya?" he growled. "Think you can stand up here and talk shit about old Nige? After everything I fackin' did for ya, an all. Ungrateful cow."

Katie squirmed frantically, her fingers digging below the rope as she desperately tried to find purchase. The sight of her struggling only seemed to fuel Nigel's tongue. It curved upwards across his top lip, then dipped down to coat the bottom in a slug-trail of hot saliva.

His hand went to the buckle of his belt. He glanced around, either to make sure he didn't have an audience, or hoping he had. If it was the latter, he was disappointed. The mob had completely dispersed now. Other than Nigel, Katie was completely alone.

"Nigel, don't," Katie said. She'd intended for it to come out like a command, but there was a pleading tone to it, instead. "Just don't, OK?"

With a series of tugs, Nigel removed his belt. He held the end without the buckle and gave the belt a few experimental swishes. The idea of beating Katie with it clearly appealed to him, but he had other things in mind.

He tossed the belt aside and sucked in his gut as he unfastened the button of his trousers.

"Nigel, fuck off," Katie warned. She kicked out at him, but he dodged and responded with a sharp cackle of glee.

"What's the matter?" he asked her. "I thought you said I had a kiddie's cock? If that's the case, then what you worried about? You won't hardly feel a thing."

He dodged another kick, then lunged forwards, his sausage fingers finding the front of Katie's shirt. Buttons pinged off as he tore the shirt open, exposing her bra. Nigel gave a groan of approval, his hand pressing against the erection growing in his pants.

"I take it back, sweetheart," he told her, whistling through his teeth as he ogled her chest. "Them tits of yours ain't half bad."

He stepped forward again, his hands grabbing. "Now, let's get a proper look at 'em."

———

"HOLD ON. I'm positive it's one of these buttons," Boris mumbled. "Bloody technology. Made by the Japs, probably. Gadgets, and whatnot. Devious-minded buggers the lot of them."

Sexton had twisted his head just enough to be able to draw in a breath without drowning. The gun was still touching the back of his head, but there was less pressure on it now that Boris was distracted. It was a tickle through his hair, and nothing more.

"Ah. Yes. Here we are. Camera. Bingo," Boris said. "I was looking for the word, 'camera,' but it's just a little picture of one. That explains it."

There was a soft *bleep* from the phone in Boris's hand. Sexton managed another breath, which helped ease the fire burning in his lungs.

"There, now we can film your final… Wait. That's me. Why is it showing me? I don't want it to show me," Boris said, sounding increasingly exasperated. "Do I just…?"

Click.

Boris tutted. "No. That's not… Christ, that's not a good angle. I'm all chins. How do I delete…? Wait. I see it."

He gave a little 'Hurrah' of triumph.

"Rear camera. That's the boy. It's a little twisty icon. Now I can…"

His face vanished from the screen and was replaced by a view of a puddle. The end of the gun was visible right at the edge of the image, but one thing that wasn't visible was Sexton.

Boris lowered the phone a few inches and peered over the top of it, in case it was playing tricks on him.

"Oh… bugger," he managed to eject, before a scalpel was buried in his arm and the rifle went clattering onto the wet tarmac.

———

KATIE CAUGHT Nigel a glancing blow on the side of his horrible fucking melon-head with her tied-together fists. He hissed angrily and cracked a backhand across her cheek that wrenched her around and dug the noose in tighter against her throat.

The edges of the world became feathered by darkness. She tried to lash out again, but missed, and could only watch in a wheezing, breathless silence as Nigel's trousers slipped down to his ankles.

She tried to scream, but the rope was too tight, too constricting. She wished she hadn't sent Sexton away. Wished he would come back around the corner. Wished he'd put a stop to this before it went any further.

Nigel's hands were suddenly on her belt. She felt his hot breath on her neck, saw his piggy-eyes bulge hungrily as he forged his fat fingers down the front of her jeans and inside her underwear. His red-face glistened in the rain, although it might just as easily have been sweat.

She flashed her teeth, trying to take a chunk of out him, but the rope stopped her reaching him. He sniggered at her, a low, grunting snort that made the horror of what was about to happen seem suddenly all the more real.

"Keep it up, sweetheart," he told her. "It'll be more fun if you—Ow!"

Something struck him on the back of his thighs. He grimaced and spun clumsily around, his trousers still around his ankles.

A scrawny girl in oversized clothing stood on the platform, Nigel's belt in her hand. "What the fack is this?" Nigel spat.

"Bad… man," said the girl, her hands shaking as she clutched the belt.

"You don't know the fackin' half of it," Nigel hissed. He moved to grab for Marta, but Katie's hands looped over his head from behind and the rope holding them together drew tight across Nigel's throat.

He tried to jump free, but the tangle of his trousers sent him into a sprawl.

Katie hung on, heaving him back towards her, fighting against the grip of the noose. She couldn't get so much as a sip of air now, and the darkness was closing like a tunnel around her.

But she couldn't let go. She wouldn't. Not in this lifetime.

Nigel lashed out with his fists, raining blow after blow on her sides. She ignored them. Ignored everything. Just focused on pulling and squeezing and not passing out.

The next few blows were solid.

The few after that, less so.

Nigel gagged and wheezed, his bloodshot eyes fixed on Marta. Katie wanted to tell her to turn away, to not look, but the words couldn't come.

Nigel's legs wobbled. Katie held on for as long as she could until the strain of holding him up was too much for her neck to take, and she was forced to let him go.

He slumped onto the wooden floor, his head *cracking* on one of the planks. Katie stood on the back of one unmoving thigh, relieving some of the pressure around her throat. She thrust her hands towards Marta, her eyes wide and pleading.

Marta retreated quickly and fled down the steps. Katie tried to call after her, but her throat was still too constricted.

A drumbeat pounded inside her head. Her lungs cramped up. Katie's eyes closed over, and she felt her legs shake as they finally gave way.

―――――

FORMER FOREIGN SECRETARY, Boris Johnson, screamed as he hurtled through the air and smashed, upside-down, into the side of the skip. The scalpel was still buried in his arm, the collision having driven it a clear two inches deeper into his wobbly flesh.

"N-no, please. Please!" Boris sobbed, dragging his generous torso through the dirt and the puddles as

Sexton advanced. "Don't do this. I implore you. I *beseech* you!"

He made a grab for his sock, and got his fingertips to a knife he kept hidden there before Sexton kicked the hand away.

"Don't even think about it," Sexton growled, drops of rain dripping from the end of his nose. "You did this. You and your fucking friends. You broke this country."

"We're fixing it. It's going to be even better!" Boris whimpered. "I swear. It'll just take some time to smooth out the wrinkles."

"Shut up!" Sexton barked, making Boris jump.

There was another moment of frantic fumbling from the straw-haired former Tory frontbencher. The phone in his hand gave a *click* and flashed in Sexton's face.

"Th-there! I got you. They'll know who you are," Boris babbled. "You'd better let me go, or they'll be after you. There… There'll be nowhere for you to run to. Nowhere for you to go."

His face twisted up with rage. "They'll find you. If you think you know suffering now, then just wait! You hear me? Just wait!"

Sexton bent and pulled the scalpel from Boris's arm with a damp *schlop*. While Boris was busy screaming, he took the phone from Boris's hand, then slipped it into his pocket.

"It's too late. It uploads automatically," Boris wheezed. "They'll come for you. They'll kill you."

Sexton shrugged. "Then good luck to them."

Catching Boris by the hair, he forced his head back and took aim with the scalpel.

"Wait! Wait!" Boris cried, in a voice that was distinctly un-Boris. "I'm not him. I'm not him. I'm a decoy."

Sexton hesitated.

"Bollocks."

"It's true! I swear, mate. I swear. I'm not him. I just look like him."

"You look *exactly* like him," Sexton pointed out.

"Surgery, innit? There's three of us. We do these events. He doesn't come out for them. Too scared of the Moggies or the Corbynites or whoever catching him. He sends us."

Sexton looked the man up and down. "I don't buy it."

"Me hair. Check me hair. The roots. They're dark, see? I ain't him. I ain't him. I ain't nobody!"

Sexton tore out a handful of the yellow crop in one swift, sudden yank, drawing another scream from the man in the suit. He studied the end.

Brown. Dark brown.

"Fuck!"

"See? See, I told you. I ain't him," the fake Boris wheezed. "I'm just doing a job, that's all. I'm just doing my job."

Sexton nodded slowly. "Just doing your job," he muttered. "Right."

He clicked his tongue against the back of his teeth a few times. "OK, here's what we're going to do. We're going to send him a message."

"Of course. Of course, anything you want," the impostor wheezed. "Just tell me what you want me to say."

"Sorry, you misunderstand," said Sexton. His hand tightened on the knife. "You *are* the message."

———

KATIE GASPED awake as air flooded her lungs in deep, desperate gulps.

She lay on the gallows platform, the rope hanging

limply beside her, the end of it clumsily sheared away. Nigel lay crumpled beneath her, his eyes wide, bloodshot and staring, his face a road map of burst capillaries on a terrain of dark, pock-marked purple.

Good riddance.

Katie spent an enjoyable few seconds punching several shades of shit out of his bloated corpse before it dawned on her that her hands were no longer bound.

She looked around to find Marta standing by the top step, a worried expression on her face, a huge fucking machete in her hand. Marta gave Katie an anxious little wave, then collapsed onto the platform, buried her face in her hands, and sobbed.

Katie's arms and legs shook as she crawled over to the girl. She slumped beside Marta, wincing as she draped an arm across her slender shoulders.

"It's OK. We're OK," Katie assured her. "We're safe. Thanks to you."

Marta raised her eyes from her hands and peered solemnly up at Katie. "Bad men?"

"No more bad men," Katie told her. "The bad men are all gone."

The wood creaked behind them. Katie grabbed for the machete, but Marta was already spinning with it, screeching like a banshee as she swung it around in a wide, scything arc.

"Jesus *Christ*!" spat Sexton, stumbling down the stairs in time to avoid being decapitated. The machete blade cut deep into the wooden frame of the gallows with a *thunk*.

The look of shock on his face was only beaten by the one on Marta's.

"She could've cut my head off. Who the hell gave the kid a giant knife?" Sexton asked.

Katie laughed. It hurt, but it felt good. She held up a hand and Sexton took it.

"Haven't you heard? All the cool kids have them, these days," she said, grimacing as she was heaved up onto her feet. "They're this year's fidget spinners."

Sexton frowned. "What's a fidget spinner?"

Katie shot Marta a sideways look and rolled her eyes. "I can see we're going to have our work cut out for us."

Despite having no idea what Katie had said, Marta rolled her own eyes, then joined Katie in shaking her head in Sexton's general direction.

Katie batted Sexton's hand away when he tried to help her down the stairs, and indicated that he should help Marta, instead. Marta took his hand without hesitation, her grip tightening as far as it would go. Sexton wrapped his fingers all the way around hers, and led her down the steps onto solid ground.

"You, uh, you probably don't want to look at that," he said, turning her away from a pile of bodies. "Or that," he added, realising she was now staring directly as a smear of organs and bloody tyre tracks.

He put his hand over her eyes. "In fact, probably best if you don't look anywhere for a while. At least until we're out of town."

Katie removed the remains of the noose from her neck and tossed the rope aside. "We're still going, then?"

Sexton shrugged. "I mean, you can always stay if you'd prefer."

"Tempting," said Katie. She tapped a fingernail against her teeth. "But no. You talked me into it. I'll come."

She set off limping. Sexton let her get almost thirty feet before loudly clearing his throat.

"I was going to take the ambulance…" he said, jabbing a thumb towards the armoured vehicle. "It's pretty conspicuous, but, on the other hand, it's pretty much a tank."

Katie regarded the vehicle. "It's a long walk to Scotland."

"That it is," Sexton confirmed. He opened the door and helped Marta into the middle seat, then clambered into the driver's seat beside her.

The door on the other side opened and Katie climbed in. She looked around the cabin, opened the glove box, then rocked in her chair. "It's pretty nice," she said. "A bit *Mad Maxy*, but not bad."

She leaned back and put her feet up on the dash. "Yes, I could get used to this."

Sexton gave a single throaty, "Ha!" then looked down at Marta. "Seat belt."

He pulled his own on to demonstrate, then watched her until she had fastened herself in.

"Seat belt," she said in an accent Sexton was sure would, ultimately, get them all killed.

Still, that was a problem for another day.

"Did you get him?" Katie asked. "Did you get Boris?"

Sexton turned the key in the ignition and the ambulance roared into life. The gearbox complained as he crunched the stick into reverse.

"Yeah," he said. "I got him."

And with that, he reversed onto the Esplanade, exploded a few corpses, and headed north.

Epilogue

He sat on his throne in what had once been the library, licking chicken grease from his fingers as he gazed out across the immaculate grounds. He wiped his hands absent-mindedly on his Tudor-style smock, watching the drab afternoon sky meander across the rooftops of Oxford.

As he watched the gathering clouds, his mind turned to thoughts of his next meal. He finished the degreasing of his fingers by rubbing them against his tights, modelled closely on those worn by King Henry VIII himself. An admirable chap, he thought. A little eccentric, perhaps, but where was the harm in that.

He considered calling for more food but decided he should attend to his other appetites first. Spread the love, so to speak. He'd have some alcohol. A few lines of coke. That new serving wench they'd confiscated from Rees-Mogg, perhaps. She was a bit more robust around the hips than he generally approved of, but that would surely only make her more grateful for his affections, however brief and demeaning they may be.

Yes. Drink, drugs, and debauchery were all most

certainly on the cards, although he hadn't yet decided the order in which he'd be partaking. Perhaps one of his advisors could help. One of the back-benchers, perhaps. Or that dreadful Scottish man with the beard who'd been exiled after the wall had gone up. God, what was his name?

He rang the bell that was attached to the arm of the ornately carved throne and waited for someone to attend. The door opened more quickly than he'd anticipated, and a sturdy chap in his late-forties hurried in. From the expression on his face, it was clear something was bothering him. It wouldn't do just to let him blurt it out, though.

"Ah. Tugendhat," he said, snapping off a lazy salute. "The very man."

Tom Tugendhat, a former Army officer turned Conservative MP, returned a salute straight out of a textbook. "Lord Johnson. We have a problem," he said.

Boris Johnson, Grand Lord of the South West, waved a hand dismissively. "Yes, yes. First thing's first. Scottish bloke. What's his name again. Beard. Queer, I think. Got the look about him, anyway."

"David Mundell," said Tugendhat.

"Yes! That's the fellow," Boris cried. His voice echoed around the delicate carvings of the library ceiling. "Is he still around?"

Tugendhat gave a curt shake of his head. "You had him killed, m'lord."

Boris straightened in surprise. "Did I?"

"Last week. You burned him."

"Was that him?" Boris said. "Goodness, I barely recognized him. He was looking well."

"Was, sir, yes," said Tugendhat. He cleared his throat. "You should see this, m'lord."

He held out an iPad, which Boris eyed with suspicion. A photograph was on screen. It showed a grainy image of bearded man standing in the rain, his eyes blazing hatred straight down the camera lens.

"This one looks like trouble," Boris remarked.

"Indeed, sir," Tugendhat confirmed. "This was taken earlier today by one of the stand-ins. He was down in Weymouth, attending a Reckoning."

Boris shrugged. "And? So, he took a photo of some angry looking chap. What's the big problem?"

"Two other pictures arrived in the cloud storage shortly after," Tugendhat said. He swiped the screen. It showed an uncanny likeness of the man in the throne with a gaping smile where his throat should have been.

"Christ. That's eerie, isn't it?" Boris snorted. "Really catches you off guard. Bloody creepy the way he… And, oh, he's dead. How did that happen?"

"Someone cut his throat, m'lord."

"Yes, well, I can see *that*, obviously. Who was it? That other chap?" Boris asked.

"We believe so," said Tugendhat. "The whole Reckoning turned into a massacre. Several Bojos were killed. Many supporters, too."

"Bugger. That's unfortunate," said Boris, although there wasn't a lot of feeling behind it.

Tugendhat shifted uncomfortably, like he didn't want to be the bearer of the upcoming news. "And he, uh, he left a message, sir."

Boris frowned. "What sort of message?"

Tugendhat flicked to the next image. It showed a man's bare chest. Blood had been smeared across the rolls of fat and the flabby man-tits. It read:

We're taking our country back.

Boris leaned back in his throne. "I see. And who is he? This man? Do we know?"

Tugendhat shook his head. "We don't, m'lord."

"Then I suggest you get a fucking move on and find out, Tom," said Boris. He gripped the arms of his throne so tightly that his nails scratched grooves in the wood. "Because either that bastard's head is on a spike by the end of the week, or yours is."

Tugendhat gave a single nod of understanding, then saluted again. "Yes, m'lord. Very good, m'lord."

"Dismissed," said Boris, ushering him towards the door with a snap of his hand.

With a crisp about-turn, Tugendhat made for the exit. He had almost reached it when Boris stopped him in his tracks.

"Oh, and Tom?"

"Yes, m'lord?"

"Fetch me that fat girl we took from Mogg, would you? There's a good chap." He ran his fingers through his scarecrow's head of blonde hair and grinned, showing his yellow teeth. "Oh, and bring me another chicken."

Printed in Great Britain
by Amazon